ZOLITUDE

Zolitude

STORIES

Paige Cooper

A JOHN METCALF BOOK

BIBLIOASIS
WINDSOR, ONTARIO

Library and Archives Canada Cataloguing in Publication

Cooper, Paige
[Short stories. Selections]
    Zolitude / Paige Cooper.

Short stories.
Issued in print and electronic formats.

ISBN 978-1-77196-217-9 (softcover).--ISBN 978-1-77196-218-6 (ebook)

    I. Title.

PS8605.O6715A6 2018   C813'.6   C2017-906995-0
                                               C2017-906996-9

Readied for the press by John Metcalf
Copy-edited by Emily Donaldson
Typeset by Chris Andrechek
Cover designed by Gordon Robertson
Cover image by Kim Keever

Published with the generous assistance of the Canada Council for the Arts, which last year invested $153 million to bring the arts to Canadians throughout the country, and the financial support of the Government of Canada. Biblioasis also acknowledges the support of the Ontario Arts Council (OAC), an agency of the Government of Ontario, which last year funded 1,709 individual artists and 1,078 organizations in 204 communities across Ontario, for a total of $52.1 million, and the contribution of the Government of Ontario through the Ontario Book Publishing Tax Credit and the Ontario Media Development Corporation.

PRINTED AND BOUND IN CANADA

For Olive

Contents

Zolitude

Simona will not come, so I go alone up the icy steps to the wine bar to find Lars sitting in tableau, dressed like a banker or a dean in a gold Windsor knot and blue shirt, white at cuff and collar, drinking a cappuccino with one knuckle through the cup's ring hole. These days our free hours are spent in blackout. Daylight shows up to eat its lunch over our desks, then leaves. Otherwise, we and time are left to manage ourselves. If this were the morning dark Lars would have a newspaper, but it's evening and his work is laid aside; here's a man who sits and reviews the day's developments with clarity and logic. When Simona first introduced me to Lars, I thought: here is a man I would try to please if I worked under him. If he were my physician, I might lie about my habits.

I linger in the entryway, hang my overcoat beside his, unwind and rewind my scarf, fish my phone out of my purse and face it blankly. The room is bright and vacant. Two women confess to each other in Russian in the corner.

The attendant behind the pine counter looks familiar but greets me formally—he is my age, probably we attended a school together at one point or another—and I wish he would retreat somewhere while I do this instead of standing there in his black shirt imagining Lars and me into a gummy internet affair coalesced, or some other private obscenity, when actually I am not even the person in this, I am just the one who is here.

"Simona is late?" Lars can't help himself; he looks out to the sleety sidewalk.

"No," I say. "She won't come."

He totters his cup in its saucer. One red blemish has developed high on his forehead. His skin's withered. Of course he isn't sleeping. How could he not have anticipated this from Simona, whose standard of callousness or cowardice expresses itself hourly? But of course he hoped she would overcome herself to be here. Simona, who is currently curled in the sunless suite of her parents' house in the Silent District, telling everyone she's terrified.

I blind-order a burgundy from the server—Dzintars is the name I now remember; a painter, visible with the artists' union—as he comes to stand by. I am hungry but I'll eat at home as it's doubtful Lars will want to pay like he usually does when we're three, though he's not a banker or a dean but a preacher, or actually an artist, and very broke.

Simona is at her family's home, and I'm here with her ring in my change purse. Lars' cappuccino is a pillow of foam at the bottom of his cup.

"So," Lars sighs. "In that case."

There's only one concept of ending that's of relevance here, in the Wednesday afterdark, just minutes or years after I approved him—so flattering how she insisted

I convene my own tribunal, how she implied I had some expertise—so she could abandon me.

"She says she's afraid."

Sympathy softens him. He has misunderstood.

Yesterday Simona issued summons, giving her parents' address instead of the tiny, tall apartment over Lačplēša she shared with Lars. She answered the door in leather slippers and bare legs, her face puffed and greasy. We sat together on her loveseat. She said, "I woke up in the dark but I couldn't move. For five minutes, not my arms or legs. I was a corpse. I didn't know where he was. He wasn't beside me. I listened for him. I listened, but I couldn't move and I was so afraid as I listened that I would hear him coming."

Then she laid out for me her various proofs: a documentary Lars liked about a man who ate a prostitute; the dream she had last year where he drilled holes up her arms, gore ellipses from wrists to elbows; a picture he sent her of a dead doe he found while visiting his mother in the Swedish countryside. She left Lars that night, and now he sits across from me, looking like an American man of business, honest and canny, though with an unusual tolerance for feelings and their ambiguity.

"She is too afraid of you," I clarify.

"That is absurd. She's spoiled," Lars says, just as Dzintars approaches to embellish my glass. I glance up, and Dzintars meets my eye so as to register that he is noting all this, possibly on my behalf, possibly for his own records. Riga is unbearably tiny. I accept the millimetre of wine. Dzintars retreats. I sip. The Russian women begin speaking to each other again.

"What does she think?" Lars says. He is curved forward, his hands hinge the table's edge. "What is this

11

delusion? That I have been violent? What has she quali-
fied as violence?"

I shake my head. I open my change purse, I peck
through the sentims. The wedding band, when I lay it on
the table, is a bolt-cut lock.

In the afternoons I am occupied rowing archival rifts in the
national library, twenty years under construction and still
unfinished but at least open, now, partially, if not to the
public then at least to us neediest academics, sickly bats of
erudition. My thesis, on the city's women and their labour,
is also very, very late. Every time I meet a woman she has
some new strategy for getting money. Money is got from
men. Today I leave as it gets dark, thirty pounds of foreign
photocopies in my backpack, and walk across the Stone
Bridge to the old town. All the tourist shops—amber and
handwoven wool—are quiet, the restaurants empty except
for bartenders better left undisturbed. The whole world
knows this city is cheap, but even so, falling in and out of
darkness like this will make you dizzy. Rooks circle the
blue-bricked churches. An old woman walks ahead of me
with a bag of fish guts. Some cats have already spotted her;
they butt her ankles like bulls.

In the dressing room of a Scandinavian boutique I
model a twill dress, a dusty-rose mid-calf pantsuit and a
slutty little ivory blouse, taking pictures of my cocked hips
in the liar mirror. I will send these to Inese, with whom
I have been flirting since before she left for Istanbul. It's
unclear if she knows I am flirting, though we did finger
each other last June in the five a.m. daylight on the steps
to the river. Everything was reversed then. In summer,
each one of us is our own twin. I change my bra for the

blouse. Black under white. I take a picture. Then remove the blouse and bra, wear just the suit. One golden button on the labial pink triangles bare skin, navel to collarbones. I'm a little delirious. My bloodstream's hotsprung, my legs weak, my head weak. I never stop thinking of this girl Inese, not really; turn in the giddy middle dark of nighttime to ask my phone if she's sent her semi-weekly phrase. I twist my torso and adjust the phone's bleary eye. My skin is saturated. I kick my backpack out of the frame. I cut my own head off. I take dozens. I resolve to let them cool before I send them. I resolve to send none of them. I flip through them. They are all terrible. I will delete them. Especially the one with the peak of my nipple in silhouette, my fingers dipped in the waistline of these half-split trousers. The curl of pubic hair made public. My hand lost in the hole. But then, look, I have pressed the button. It is sent.

I push my phone into a deep crevice of my backpack. I will never check it ever again because what if she responds? And what if she doesn't? I abandon the dressing room in disarray, flap out of the shop without meeting the salesgirl's eye.

I met Inese in the summertime, when she DJed at the place where the local half-hookers take their tourists dancing. I went there every night with my notebook and phone, pestered girls into interviews by buying them drinks and complimenting their clothing. I was firm then, my voice steady, my palms dry. Not all of the resulting material was transcribable, with the dance floor and the drunks in the background. My advisor cringes, but I stand by my methodology.

All the women I interviewed were young, like Simona and Inese are young, because we are all so rigorous about achievement in our youth here. They take gifts from tourists and they study law and they curate galleries. And they're not just rigorous but beautiful, as our beauty is something the city is known for and a standard to which we resentfully and sincerely strive. My darling Simona has her dark bramble and aristocrat nose, and Inese was built to adorn a Jugendstil façade, sword in hand and hounds at heel. Last summer I had just turned twenty-seven and had begun to feel wise. I started to smile so that the right kind of lines would settle. The young women asked my opinion. Their faces gleamed like mermaid faces. My opinion was and is that there are no men anyways. My own brother, an architect, moved to New York City, where he embarrassed his new friends by passing casual bribes.

I live on a barge moored permanently to the cement pilings of a municipal park midstream in the Daugava. There's a hotplate in the bathroom. I shower at the university gym. The city installed a special mailbox for me, but I lost the key, and the landlord, Nikolaj, who personally hauled up the half-sunk boat from the bottom of the river, where it had rotted since one occupation or another, snorted when I requested that he request the city issue a replacement. I receive one letter a year; the rest are his. Still, I pull the little pieces out through the holes at the bottom of the box. I have to tear them apart. The bigger slips I fish out from the drop slot using my key and long fingers. Some women are born with archer's bodies; I was born with witch's fingers. They take up tennis. I took up expert masturbation and lettermail retrieval.

Tonight, government letters for Nikolaj. And—wonder!—a postcard from Inese in Istanbul. A message from the Inese who has not seen the picture of my fingers down trousers I do not own. I pull the card out in crumpled halves and then piece it together on the boardwalk's frost.

Lovely, you'd hate the men/weather here, all ugly. I miss the fog coming up the steps off the river. My hands never smell of you anymore. What do you do without me? Have I ever been apart from you? xxxi

I don't allow any rejoicing. I don't stand in the dark with the frozen fog icing me to state statue, the river on all sides, the barge lit up behind me like a lily-pad palace, so chest-burst with happiness that tears are maybe falling from the sides of my eyes as I tilt up at the overcast sky's belly, ridged orange and black and now swirling. I don't reread twelve times, or thump down lightheaded on the damp-iced dock to stare at the river, my glossy enemy, victorious.

To the south, the Stone Bridge is a promenade of gas-lamped arches, wide and low, with sickles still stuck to the sides. To the north, the Shroud Bridge is red-eyed at the peak, like a malevolent queen, with its own idling suicide officer at watch every night. I am moored between them, and tonight the Shroud is strung like a chamber orchestra. It's a tradition for newlyweds to lovelock their hearts to the swoop of its finest cables. Over the years the padlocks have built up like chainmail. In the right combination of sun and rain I've seen them knotted like dew on a spider's dragline. If I dredged the river for my mail key, I'd pull up ten thousand watery promises.

Nights when I come home too late to sleep—like the night I came home stinking of Inese—I gather a half-dozen coats and sweaters from the tarred linoleum and sit out on the upper deck, eating candy. On those nights I can't look too closely at the water for fear it will look back. The river is deep and baleful, and we mistrust each other. For instance: my suspicion that one day it will buckle the Shroud Bridge's knees, locked as they are against its black push, with legs ribbed like knit stockings that collect a lace of hungry ice at mid-thigh. That ice follows nightmare physics: the plates don't form flat, but fold through six dozen thaws, clutter like discarded books along the concrete bank. In my breakwater everything is smooth, you couldn't drop a body through it. But in my nightsweats the barge floats untethered down the river, toward the open sea, under collapsed bridge decks, its helm holed by icebergs, sinking as it glides. And as our feet splash the gushing water, we see—I and my mother or Simona or whomever else I am dreaming with—that the only way to shore is leaping across a dissolving course of ice floes. Slick as glass, the floes teeter with us on them, and our knees burn as we slide to our waists, our ribs. We kick, and cut our clinging palms. The devils in these nightmares are toothed whales, white and black and also just white, in water so cold it's blue with its own light. They seize our ankles with their sawteeth and whirlpool us down the nightling league to the river bottom. They hold us there.

When my brother—wide-shouldered, short, and handsome as a hotblood—still lived in the city, we would make sulky bartenders open our beer bottles on late Tuesdays. By midnight I'd be crying and he'd be holding my face in his hands and licking his thumbs to clear the dripping black from my undereyes. Being in love with him was a natural state I returned to every time he smiled sideways at me. One time, old friends of our father's came in. A mathematician and a bassoonist. Great minds, shaking drunks. My brother turned his back on me and spoke to them as men. This shielded me from their slurring. I read the labels on the liquor bottles. The bassoonist went to the toilet, and fell up the stairs. He didn't rise. "You're his friend, aren't you?" my brother said to the mathematician. "Help him." Everyone starves for the love of men, even men themselves.

On my dock, I clutch Inese's postcard, adorned frontside with a fogged picture of a craggy summer castle, squirrel it into my pockets and vow never to respond.

Later, I buzz Simona's gate with a casual bunch of peach-mouthed flowers. Simona grew up in the Silent District among the façades and flags of the embassies, while my parents still live in a Soviet suburb halfway between here and the sea: Zolitude, where last year a roof collapsed and killed forty shoppers as they weighed their options for dinner.

Simona's mother opens the tall wooden door behind the ironwork. She looks at the flowers and says, "Do you know, Ms. Berzina, what's wrong with her?"

"These are questions one can't answer," I say.

"Will you tell her, please, that we would like her to join us for dinners if she must live here, and also that she will answer her own door?"

"Certainly," I say.

"It is very nice to see you again. Please come in from the cold, by the way." Simona's mother unlatches the wrought iron and steps aside to allow me into the dark-glassed entry. She disappears while I remove my boots. I descend the narrow stairwell to Simona's flat, where Simona peers around her own door with her mother's countenance.

"Who let you in? My mother? Does she know to not let Lars in? What if he comes here? Tell her she has to call the police if he comes."

"He won't come," I say. "And she requests you answer the door."

"Ha." Simona has never answered her own door. Her suite is ivory and lamp-lit, bare but fabricked with furs from the trapper at the Christmas market, the one who sells fox faces in bundles, each one five lats, latched with a leather thong through the buttonhole eyeslits.

"Why are you so romantic?" Simona sighs as she takes the flowers, which I selected from the row of bright, glass-walled booths at the north end of the park. The vendors stay open all night, even through the grave-bottom of winter. You see them sleeping in parkas behind their rose racks. The men still left in this city know the time for begging absolution is always at hand.

I settle my bag by her loveseat and sit, hungry, knowing there's no chance she'll have any food here. She used to brag that she only eats to prevent hangovers and appease men who want to buy her things. For at least a year with Lars she became peckish and ruminative. Her breasts swelled up.

She folds beside me. "Tea?" she says. Her hair is dark, dried sideways because she's recently chopped it blunt by her own hand; actually, since I last saw her. It's still more elegant than mine, which I dye an ashy white that steadily yellows in the river water. I paste it flat over my forehead, where it crackles.

"That would be nice," I say, just to see if she'll move.

She doesn't, except to place her temple on my shoulder. "What did he say?"

I ponder the flowers, which she has dropped in a dry pitcher. "He didn't understand."

"He doesn't need to understand," she seethes. "He knows already. He made me figure it out."

"Figure what out?"

"That he wants to murder me." Simona pulls away, then comes back to toy at my jacket's buttons. She slips one hand inside. Her thumb traces the undercurve of my breast.

I lean my head back. She raises her nose to my throat. I turn my face away to yawn. "He does?"

"You should be on my side," she says, and kisses my chin. She leans into me and twists my hair, and for a second we are back in my campus office and her careless paper is on my desk with a red six on it and her tights are around her knees and I'm licking her hairless, but then I pull back, I stop this. I remove myself. In fact, she was the one who taught me, by example, to remove myself from the whorl.

I say, "You should try to be sane. You'll regret doing it this way."

"He will regret it," she says, but her voice disintegrates.

Two years ago we sat here in this room, twinned on this loveseat, and she said, "I've been seeing this man." When her phone shuddered she smiled at it idiotically and took it away with her. I sat here, full of hate. But then, when I set the ring on the table before him, my hand was hers, my eyes were hers, and I was the vessel of all her powers. He is the enemy and we are destroying him.

On Independence Night my barge is the most desirable location in the city, which is awash with a citizenry who marched for hours in lit procession to limn castle walls with red-glassed candles, and prayed in the cantata wings of every church shrieking, *God, your country is on fire!*, and bestrewed with flowers the rifle-armed soldiers who decorate the most important of our monuments, from which we launched a burning catafalque into the river. At midnight, these same citizens line the river's concrete banks and the interior walks of both Stone and Shroud, while my landlord and his friends stand on the barge's upper deck and watch the workers light the cannons from which fireworks are shot skyward. Here we stand liquored in the neural core of the explosions, which are granular and immense. "Like Germany in forty-four, huh?" Nikolaj calls, gleeful. The fiery shards are heavy, and fall hissing around us. Across the river, loudspeakers project the national anthem, and all our voices lift in high duty. Every one of us sings gloriously.

Inside the upper deck of the barge is my home, with a bed that splits apart like kindling and the rest an attic of dusty, dried-up paints and paintings. Most of them I've turned toward the walls. Downstairs is the smooth-floored gallery and a toilet. Below that, storage. Nikolaj's contemporaries—artists, importers, some bureaucrats, poets, a few drunks, et cetera—assume I am something like an intern or a social climber. They ask me if there's more to drink, and I open bottles. Dzintars from the wine shop, wearing a fur hat, holds out his glass and smiles delicately at me. Nikolaj is variously important. His women friends take me for cunning. One of them asks, "But should I introduce you as Nikolaj's girlfriend?"

"Certainly," I say. Perhaps this will discount my rent. I look across the room to my landlord: he is as old as Lars, but bearded and scowling, with rings on all his fingers. Fucking him would be a laborious performance, but not as laborious as forgiving him his personality—all of his women friends have been fucked by him—and I am not an empiricist, nor his friend. It's impossible. This is a city in which Inese once licked my fingers, kneeling.

Before she left me here, Inese invited me to a festival afterparty in the port district, where the Naïve Art Museum used to display its ugly wares and now where once or twice a year a small cruise ship full of Finns or footballers will dock. I walked down a long road wet with puddles turned to pond, and I carried my lighter in fist to mark my presence to the cars sneering down the laneway in the utter black, and to provide a floating fairy reflection to cue myself before bogging ankle-deep in marshwater. At the warehouse door, a man reviewed my knapsack, which carried three too many books to be comfortable. Inside, a warren of stairwells and galleries. One room a wading pool of dead leaves, smelling honestly of autumnal possibility. Blouses hung from wires, their pricetags fluttering: the room belonged, actually, to a certain Scandinavian boutique, and a certain familiar salesgirl stood guard. I slid away from her glance. Downstairs, there was a carousel, and dancers circling their hips on a loading dock, and everyone was standing in clumps in their parade finery. At each of the ballroom's three bars the menus, printed in Cyrillic, offered a different but entirely crystalline swill. Inese manifested with a tumbler in hand just as I decided I was too afraid, and could therefore order nothing.

"What is it?" I asked her.

"Vodka, they call it," she said, leaning back from the hip. She, like everyone, was wearing a clutter of items—horse hair, gemstones, phials of liquid—that defied theme but twisted emotion. Such items I would not consider buying, much less wearing out among hostile eyes. All eyes were hostile. Women continually came up to her. One barely dipped her tiny paw into my cold palm, and it took me long minutes to condense her air into pre-planned malice. Yet Inese was warm to this woman with the boxer jowls, and admired her before me. She excused herself to the other side of the room, where a circle accreted around her, and yet another blonde I didn't know continually leaned in to touch shoulders, one hand on Inese's arm, one heel floating, her head laughing back in howled victory. This was when it became clear that loving her would beggar me.

Even earlier than that, I was present when Simona first met Lars. We attended one of his sermons. It was listed as a lecture, and located in an art gallery. We threaded under the streets, through the angled passages where the old women sell their trash, and emerged in the market stalls where the glass-walled park vendors buy the flowers that they then resell from their crystal huts in the city centre at madder prices. The gallery itself, past the guts of the fish market, was new, birch and whitewashed plaster. There was the usual sparse, familiar audience. We settled, and Lars—though we did not know his name yet—had us all stand and raise our right hands. He praised Jesus. We sat again. I looked solemn, because a camera was recording the event. I've watched this video, all our soulless faces, several times since. He said:

"I suppose you believe in science, as I do. The facts around the age of our universe and the creation of our life here are incontrovertible. They are proven, they are backed up by hundreds of years of research. I grew up atheist. I grew up academic. Science is a known thing. But I also know the existence of God. When I fell in love with Him—and it was, it was like love, my beating heart, my jealousy, my lying awake at night thinking about this new Lord of mine, this Jesus Christ—I entered a paradox. I believed in science and the rational universe, as I had always done, but I had fallen in love with someone who could not exist in my own notion of the world.

"I thought I was going crazy. I researched delusion. I researched the symptoms of delusion: how, in the absence of real proof, the afflicted creates his own proof for his own outcomes, and because they're his own, he holds even more tightly to them. My proofs were my own, they did not exist for geologists, botanists, or astrophysicists; though of course I also still believed in their proofs. I had to hold this paradox in my heart. I had to live within it.

"I have two children. I do not live with their mother. They split their time between us, one week with her, one with me. The situation is not ideal. The children are unhappy. They say, because they are clever, 'We want to live with her but we also want to live with you.' But since that can't happen, it is an impossibility, they must exist in a state of anguish, between us. And so it is easiest—even best—for them to forget their mother when they are with me, and to forget me when they are with her, and love us both entirely, but separately. It is the only way to resolve the paradox," and here he paused, adding, as if to himself: "The resolution being what makes it a paradox and not a contradiction."

And then he led the congregation in a hymn. His piano playing was clunky, his voice uncertain and limited. Simona, beside me, convulsed and refused to meet my eye, afraid to guffaw. "Sing along, please," he encouraged us as he squawked. I did, quiet and conscious of our voices' power. He seemed unembarrassed to be outdone. Eventually, he stood, straightened his jacket, smoothed his hair back, and continued:

"Neuroscientists have concluded that love and fear are the only two physiologically measurable emotions. Everything else is so similar to one or the other that tests cannot distinguish further subtleties. Fear waves are short, sharp. Love is slow, deep, and long. Or maybe," he paused. "Is it the other way? Is it that fear is long? No, I mean, I'm sure. That's right. Love is slow and deep, and fear spikes. So we understand that anger is just fear, and sadness is actually love. Through the mechanism of jealousy we sometimes confuse one for the other, and think they are the same emotion, but they aren't. They are separate and absolutely singular. We feel them constantly, all the time, in doses. Often, we take them as proof of our delusions. But then, thoughts are not facts either, are they?"

After, Simona lingered. I took my coat from the rack and stood by the door. Simona spoke to him with her head cocked and her hands brushing the sides of her thighs slowly, continuously. He was seventeen years older than she was. His children were nine and six at the time. He was wearing his golden knot, his banker's suit. He was tall, and wide, but not fat. His face was round. I don't know that she wanted to have sex with him in the way she often wanted sex with people she found impressive, and if so whether it was the children or the faith that aroused her, but she swayed charmingly for him, and then later, when I learned it was him she was in love with to the point of obsession, to the point of mass exorcism, I was angry. Or, I guess, I was afraid.

I don't like to admit this, but I've purchased a plane ticket for Inese. I asked her to come back from Istanbul to visit me here. It cost two month's rent and I'm embarrassed to be so desperate, but she was embarrassed that night, admitting she's poor, which is why she has not yet come to visit me—not the city, me! We have been close lately, talking on the phone. She liked the pictures. She said which ones she liked most. I typed my credit card number one-handed into the website and asked her middle name. It's Nadège. I bought for the 11th rather than the 10th because it was better for her, even though the 10th was cheaper by forty lats.

I want her here. I need her to come and tell me to my face that she could love me, not just say it while drinking a whole bottle of wine on the phone and then passing out so I could hear her snoring softly, her breath something I stayed with a long time, trying to find the edge of sleep myself, as if we shared the same pillow. I couldn't cut the line.

I've bought flowers, white-faced and wrapped in butcher paper, but should I have? I'm not sure she'll come. This morning before she would have boarded she sent a message that said, "If I'm not on the plane it's because I'm afraid of flying." I typed a response. Did I send it? "If you're not on the plane I'll throw myself into the river." I see myself walking away from the airport, alone, holding these flowers, so I've hidden them in my purse. If I get to hand them to her, it will be with nonchalance. I will push them into her chest and roll my eyes. I am standing in the arrivals area and my ankles are trembling atop my heels. I am leaning against this pillar for stability. I am wearing a skirt but no underwear. Walking to the bus station, the wind off the river crept up my crotch and, unable to look down, I imagined the whole thing riding up, exposing my hopes to the wet-blown lamplit rush hour. There are children here in the waiting area running around with single blooms for their returning mothers. There is a thin young man in a well-cut overcoat who paces in his point-toed dress shoes, and his circles are shearing off my nerve endings. The baggage carousel is on the other side of sliding fogged glass and people stream out—I can see the crowd milling just beyond, barely—from their varied flights and I stare at them, watch for her. I know her gait, colour, height because she's burnt into me, she's still burning. I teeter, fingertips pressed to the pillar. My blood spirals through me. I slip, sideways, down a fraction. If she doesn't come, I will go home. I will cope. If she comes—no. I cannot even think it. I cannot even think of what might happen if she comes.

Spiderhole

Dusty sheathes himself in khaki against the sun and wind, kisses his wife and her girl, and drives inland on one red, day-long shot of road. On the second morning, he passes over the Annamites, his bike roaring in second up the grade, gravel hawking off the hairpins into the blue-black, the dipterocarp sea, the pit he's climbing out of. The road is empty, except for potholes and a single, starved Honda driven by a kid in a dirty t-shirt, hunting rifle slashed across his shoulders. No animal life—it's been devoured. On his right, over the scarp, the mountains are imbricate rows of corroded teeth. This place is a national park now, all of it. Protected. From who? It blows his fucking mind.

A week ago, at home on the coast, he'd parked it early at his local—Muster Point, the place he met Mimi, actually—and heard a young man talking with a Chicago accent to the pretty white girl half-asleep on his shoulder. Most of the guys in town are sick of tourists, preferring their own kind, who make no judgments, but the kid reminded Dusty of his son, and there was no one else in the place besides the bar girls with their same old patter. He twisted on his stool, propped his elbows on the bar. "Where you coming from? First time? I swear I thought I'd never come back fifty years ago, but now I'm here living like a king and no complaints." The girl raised her head, gazed balefully at him, and resettled her scarf around herself, this time over her face to keep his eyes off her. Why anyone would bring their girlfriend to this country was beyond him.

The young man said, "My dad was a marine here."

"Oh yeah? Where was he stationed? I was up north. The temple. You know it?"

"He didn't talk about it," said the young man.

"Not much to say," said Dusty, lifting his beer.

"We're going up to that temple in a few days," said the young man, looking to the corpse on his shoulder for affirmation. "It's on our list. Have you ever done the tour? They have a T-Rex."

"Good for you," said Dusty. "I gotta go back myself, one of these days."

That night he went on his computer and booked himself a bungalow. Mimi peered at the screen and snorted. "That town is shit. You want to waste your money like a tourist? I have to bring Miranda to school." He reached for her hip from his chair and smooched her denim behind. "All right by me, princess."

He finds the resort just fine. A winding stone wall; a cool green tunnel. A two-storey hexagonal restaurant open wide to the wetlands. The man at the desk is a local, with the flat, unsardonic affect that they use instead of pretending properly to care. "Good morning," he says. It's three p.m. A girl with her face painted to look worse—ink eyebrows, strawberry mouth, pimples under white cream—leads him to his bungalow, which is set by itself atop stilts, fifteen feet off the ground. The chairs and walls are woven rattan. There's a rat-sized hole gnawed in the wall beside the electrical outlet. A wide rope hammock hangs on the balcony. A water tank decked with solar panels balances high above.

"Can I get a ashtray?" he says as she hands the key to him. "Don't wanna burn the whole swamp down." He laughs. "Again." The English isn't that good around here. On the coast, men like him provide enough motivation that the bars hire private tutors for their girls.

"Ashtray," she says. "Yeah." She crunches back down the gravel path. The only other sound is the whine and drone of the insects, and the sucking movements of the grazer lizards in the mud, their bells tinkling monkishly.

Dusty lights a cigarette. Flat miles of marsh open east. The expanse is rimmed in the distance by the azure mountains, and beneath them the foliage of the trees resuming, and beneath them the insubstantial brush clumps, patches of solid-looking grass scattered with shards of neon water like holes you could drop through to another reality where the napalm's still lit. No cover, he notes.

Grazers and flyers speckle the demesne. The grazers gleam like gunmetal, hock-deep or flopped in muck, their massive haunches and pawing arms perpetually sloped head-down as they dig through weeds. Their babies, big as horses, keep close, but he's seen them fall occasionally into mud pits and bawl for a rescue their own mothers can't provide. Hadrosaurids with shovel-shaped snouts and a thousand grinding teeth. He used to watch them through his scope, uncountable herds passing the dug-in LZ. It was inevitable that some grunt would pick off a few on semi-auto so the mass would lose its vast, simple mind and flee, galumphing like frogs, wailing from their clarion crests.

The flyers are just that: green as limes, slim and indignant, graceless in the air but fast as shit when they stab for a victim. One is perched on the back of a grazer, just sitting there like a prince. Dusty's seen them up close. Those lizard-birds are big as he is. But there are so few now. "Skeleton crew," he mutters. He leaves his smushed cigarette on the table where the ashtray will go.

In the morning he orders an American breakfast where the eggs are good but the bacon is underdone and he says so to the waiter, a little guy in a green shirt, basically, "I like your thinking, bud, but you gotta burn off some of that fat. See?" He holds up the dripping strip. The waiter apologizes, takes the plate back, and returns with a brand new one, five strips, no discernible difference. Dusty shakes his head and laughs to the other guests, who ignore him, and spreads out over his yellow legal pad. He's started his memoir again. It's all been said but no one's ever said it right. He lights a cigarette and they—a Brit in pink shorts carrying a fat book on lizards; an elderly French couple with a stiff bob and a chicken wattle, respectively; and a stumpy pair of Germans all in white—clear out.

As the sun inches over to touch him he starts to sweat, and soon it's so hot he retreats to his balcony, where at least one angle of the roof creates a dark cavity for him to squat in. He's got thirty of these pads full up back home. He works on them until it's time to head to the bar, brain full of rumours nobody wants to chew on but him. On Saturdays, when Mimi's off from her job at the dealership, he takes her and her girl to the beach. The same beach where they smoked grass on R&R, the same beach where, middle of the fucking afternoon, he saw a soldier pushed out of a helicopter. Alive and handcuffed into the hard blue bay as an example to the next one who wouldn't talk. Everyone at the bar calls bullshit. The CIA wouldn't pull that on an R&R beach. The owner, Errol, tells him privately to shut his hole. All the old stories have been told to death, people only want to hear new rumours now: who's running meth over the border; whose heart gave out from all the Cialis.

Later in the afternoon the clouds ball up and spit rain. The grazers are wallowed deep in their mud pits, dunking their heads and splashing themselves with their tails, but they lumber up for the shower. There's another species, too, a long file of dryland herbivores tiptoeing along the fence at the edge of the muck, their bells chiming, their skins ginger, chestnut, golden-pink. Slenderer, these ones, with long bony necks and their fine skulls held high for dangers that died off forever ago. Dusty can't remember what they're called properly in Latin. A redneck on base swore he was gonna ride one once, fashioned a couple lassos out of his kit and got some guys to hold it down one red evening. Kid clutched on for a good six seconds before it threw him and tore in with those bastard claws. So they shot the fucker and carried the kid to the medic with his chest sucking wider and wider. Nameless kid. You never saw so many guys desperate to be noticed.

These grazers, they're just eating shrubs and they freeze when the Brit in the pink shorts goes tromping down towards them. He's got a transmitter in his hand, and a whining black buzz of a drone swoops back in from the marsh, where he'd been trying to snap the flyers. The whole cavalcade starts squawking and about-facing, the babies hopping in the mud like little morons.

"Don't like you much," Dusty calls down.

The Brit turns and shrugs, embarrassed. "Aren't very domesticated, are they?"

"Not for you, Whitey," says Dusty. "Smart fuckers know."

Come evening Dusty's still sitting on his porch, tolerating the kamikaze runs of the great black night bugs while he drinks his seventh and maybe final beer. A gecko the size of his forearm is suctioned to the slats of rattan up near the light, not moving a scale but crunching beetles and moths like apples. Its molt trails a white flag behind it. He counts the blue bumps on its new hide. Once, on base, he saw one big as an alligator out back of the piss tubes. There's bugs here that could feed that. Spiders like hub cabs, wasps the size of your cock if you're lucky.

"Well, Sylvia," he says to the gecko. It's eight p.m. and black as hell out there. "Wrap her up."

There are lights out over the wetland. White dots, then a sweep from pool to pool like a skipped stone, dissipating. Locals with flashlights and finger-thin boats out collecting giant bog snails and frogs because better the black than the murdering sun.

The crush of footsteps down his path. Multiple incoming. White searchlights flicker over the rocks, catch infernal shadows that jag and leap. They angle up and pin him.

"Jesus, you wanna watch where you're pointing those things?" He flicks on the porch bulb.

Three local kids in shorts and flip-flops, wearing headlamps. They stop to stare up at him. The one in the Batman t-shirt says, "Where you from?"

"Metropolis," says Dusty. "Where you from, Batman?"

The kids laugh at him and keep going. Dusty leans back in his chair. But then, sure enough, the platoon circles back again, smirking and glancing.

"Gotham City!" Batman calls.

"No fuckin' way," says Dusty. He taps his temple. "Nice headlamp. Wait there a second." He fumbles his own lamp off his bedside table and returns with it around his forehead. He claps his hands. "Where we headed, sarge? Let's go!" The boys flow up onto the porch to examine it. Their headlamps are splintered plastic; wires tangle down to fat D-cell batteries loaded like rifle cartridges into a bamboo tube. They take his off his head: it's a third of the size, with LED lights from the future. "No way, bucko, I need that thing." He grabs it back, misses. He's actually pretty drunk. Batman was his son's favourite. He would've bought his son a thousand flashlights if he'd asked. In the city, on R&R, boys like these whipped by faster than bats on bicycles, took the pens right out of your shirt pocket. But these kids, their auntie comes by with a bucket and yells them off and they disappear into the marsh. Hunting frogs for their families. Invisible. He cracks another beer.

On his fourth day he's filled two pads and his ass hurts from sitting in that rattan chair and there's no time like the present. Strange day, walking up to the temple, when the only way they ever used to get in or out was in a dinky C-123, sweating a tin slick as it dove down to the 500-yard airstrip that got shelled to shit every hour of every day. That dash, from the flap of the plane's armpit to the rancid three-foot trench at the edge of the tarmac, or vice versa, he survived it eight times. Now all he's got to do is pack a bottle of water and wear his hat, because the sun's like the heat off a broiler.

He pockets the little hand-drawn map his man at the front desk gave him, a copy of a copy, just an amoeba with some blurry letters. "You get this from intel?" he'd said, snorting at his own joke. The red dust stains his boots. The jungle boils up out of the swamp. Trees geyser and gush leaves. Spindly ones rocket up above the others and explode like mortars. Brittle, wrist-thick parasite vines kink and zag. He walks slow enough the flies buzz him. His new knee is good but the old one's not. Ahead, one of those bells is clanging. He turns a blind corner.

The size of it bombs his brain twice. He processes the shape in pieces. It dams the trail. The box head sways as it eyes the ground in front of its talons. It's grey-green but its throat is sooty from the jaw all the way down to the breast, like it laps oil from wells instead of water. Mean little forearms calculate in the air. It stalls, snout angled sidelong at his scent. Ten tons of muscle weaponized and taut. The air's gotten hotter. Miles behind it, the tail-tip twitches.

The man on its back clucks and prods it with his bare feet. He's got a rope whip with a couple of metal nuts on the tip in one hand, and a black machete in the other. His knees clamp around its spine, just forward of the withers. A three-foot iron pike sharpened like a bayonet hangs off a chain at his side. Behind him, a little rattan throne lurches, carrying the Brit and his binoculars and his transmitter.

"Ahoy there!" says the Brit.

Dusty gapes.

"Couldn't resist," says the Brit. "Highly recommended. The temple is quite beautiful, you know!" His drone swoops in dumb spirals overhead, behind, in front.

The lizard passes, a battleship's blistered hull, close enough to touch. Its thighs and undercarriage are wrinkled and slack, more skin than scale, matte with dirt, little twigs and dead leaves caught in a stubble of wires like burnt-off feathers. Tear tracks darken its cheek under its tiny orange eye. Chains bracelet its ankles. Its toenails are ivory. The bell around its neck jangles. Dusty is standing five feet out in the rice paddy, shin-deep in mud, on the receiving end of some ageless, godforsaken joke.

At lunch, he's sitting at his table with his legal pad. He inks a jagged line of toothy peaks. He'd never seen one. How had he forgot he never had.

"I'll get a coffee," he says to the girl. "And another beer, how about."

The Brit's out at the promontory now, under a little pagoda hung with hammocks. Whole flocks of flyers rise out of the marsh, freaked into acrobatics by that goddamn drone. The French couple are eating pasta; the man reads to the woman from a glossy screen in his hand. On the other side of the restaurant, in a garden marked Staff Only, his buddy Batman, stripped naked, brandishes a hose for an afternoon wash-down.

"Good instinct, Sarge," says Dusty, tipping his beer at the kid. The girl crinkles her forehead at him as she sets down the basket of sugar, and he waves her off. "Just talking to myself, get used to it."

Mimi teases him about it. Back when they first met she'd cock her head as she sipped the watered-down cock-tails that he shelled out for because the extra dollar went into her wages at the end of the night. He'd laugh and say, "Ignore me, princess." But soon she started lifting her eyebrows. "It's a little racist, I think," she said. "Calling us locals and yourselves foreigners. Why the big difference?" "See," said Dusty, "You get a phone and now you're going all PC on me." When he'd bought her the phone, she hadn't known what the hell to do with it. She went back to her family in the countryside and sent him a video of her little girl kicking a sandal around a dirt yard. Enough was enough. "Bring her back here," he said. Of course the mother was part of the package. Thirty bucks a month for the English school and a hundred to the mother for babysitting. Mimi's ex some Triad asshole that screwed off as soon as she got pregnant, same old story as all the girls. Her grim smirk as she'd relayed that particular anecdote, early on. True or not, her shoulders pleat tight whenever he brings up his son, his ex-wife, maybe a trip home to America one of these days. Her face closes, protecting some forlorn little thing. She needs him so badly.

His notepad lies on the table, top page twitching in the breeze off the fan. He isn't sure. He isn't exactly sure. He didn't make it to the temple. As soon as the lizard was out of sight he turned around, came back, grabbed his notepad.

"Shake it off," he orders himself. He tears out the ruined page. Got to be able to shake it off to survive life. His ex-wife suffered. You go home with lunatic vision. Everyone was insane, not just for a bit, but for real. What was real about it, the way it was a movie. He was nineteen years old. No one ever told him you could die from a nightmare. From entertainment. Everyone he's ever known bought a ticket to the pain of that war. They made the movie out of him, and he had to pay to see the insult of it. They should've made him a drug. Call it a truth serum. Call it Cialis. They call him a cliché. No one fucking knows what they think they're talking about.

Batman, soaking wet and bare-ass naked, comes up the polished wooden steps into the restaurant, grinning. None of his elders are around to chase him out. He cats between the tables, his belly round, his thing dangling, but before he reaches Dusty he spots the French couple's screen. He leans his slippery self across the woman to touch it, and the man's chair honks back and he spits something disgusted, clutching the shiny piece of shit to his breast like it's his baby.

"*Petit sauvage,*" snarls the woman.

The kid jerks away, grin confused. He averts his face from the viciousness and pads out, leaving puddles on the lacquered wood. Dusty doesn't see his grandkids anymore, mostly because his son won't let up about how he needs to watch his language, but also because he left and never went back. He came here.

"Hey lady," Dusty says to the French woman, pointing the lip of his bottle at her. "Go back to your rubber plantation, huh? *Oui?*"

There are other rumours, too. At the bar, for instance, there are regulars who say they work for a security firm, but then there's a video on the *Daily* of a man pulling a Glock on a guy driving a red Porsche and that man is his buddy Abel, who told him three days ago to keep his seat warm while he headed to the Philippines on business. Then the police come in to ask around, the same police Errol pays three hundred a month to keep the corner quiet. Then it comes down that the general who paid for the hit decided to collect the bounty on Abel, maybe offset his costs, and now Abel's supposedly gone underground, but everyone knows he's dead. And there's Errol, who, during the coup, opted out of the evacuation and holed up with his AKs and his grenades. The black sheet over the bar's ceiling is there to cover up the bullet holes. Errol, who'll never go back to Alabama because of all this new racism against whites. When Dusty asks Mimi about the elections next year, she smiles. "I love my country," is all she's ever said.

The reason no one likes tourists, with their giant orange backpacks and their tall white girlfriends, is the way they don't quite eat their sneers. Dusty knows what he looks like: paunchy and bald on a beast of a chopper with his beautiful woman riding behind, heels sparkling. These foreigners on their year-long vacations, testing their luck in the traffic, suspicious of simple kindness, imagining they're risking something, imagining their love is a genuine monument. You can tear up every inch of solid ground. You can find the tunnels that worm between people and you can even crawl in and tell yourself you've scented the other side. Sylvia, for instance, held nothing back trying to reach him. But there's no tolerating the black in there. The dirt and rot skitter into your mouth, under your collar: wet, living pressure from all angles. Don't ask your woman if she loves you. If there's a difference between science and mythology it's not perceptible within the scan of human sense. Don't wonder. That kid from the bar will or has come here with his cold, shrouded girlfriend and they will or did watch the sunrise burn up the wetlands, but that kid'll realize, eventually, that it's not heroism to crawl into someone's grave with them, and he'll dump her, eventually, in some piss-stink city or crystal-beached island in the gulf, and he'll be better off without her. Above ground. You have to save yourself from knowing what's not knowable.

The village below the temple isn't much. He's seen worse. Mimi's people, for instance. America burnt their foliage off fifty years ago and nothing ever grew back, so now they farm dirt. Little girls with tangled ponytails in Minnie Mouse dresses. This is the only place the war was ever real.

This village, though, it has rice, it has shrimp and snails, it has grazers, and it has the kind of tourists that are old and rich. It's loaded. He can tell because there's a soft-drink stand in the schoolyard, and because the temple in the middle of town is three storeys tall and brand new, red-tiled, woven with golden snakes.

Dusty strolls along, nodding and smiling at anyone who bothers to stare, sweet-talking the dogs. There are three toy shacks, and he stops to examine the balls and plastic junk, half of which are assault rifles. "What is this? You people don't sell M16s?" he asks a woman perched on a stool in the shade. She regards him, unmoved, in her blue-and-yellow floral pyjamas. He snorts. "Who do you think won this war, anyhow?" He examines the toys more closely: one is a decently realistic approximation of an AK. He buys it. He'll bring it back to the resort as a gift for the Batman. He peels off the plastic, slings the rifle over his shoulder. He pats it. "Might need this." He winks.

His man at the front desk directed him to another man, who directed him to the Tourist Center, where sure enough there's a guy who makes a call. It's eight a.m., and the sun is simmering already. Dusty lights a cigarette and catches movement in his periphery. There it is, the tyrant, bowing under a thread of electrical wire as it approaches, dead silent but for that fucking bell.

The mahout is tiny as a racetrack jockey. Old man wearing a baseball cap cinched to its last hole, an orange-and-green plaid sarong and a fatigue jacket. Everything canine and rearwards missing, dentally. Two old men, that makes them. No introductions. The lizard sidles up to a thirty-foot wood tower, where it stands still as Dusty puts his foot on its shoulder blades and levers himself into his throne. There.

They'd built the combat base crotch-to-ass against the temple at the top of the hill, twenty feet of bald rock the only nod to eight hundred years of crook-stepped holiness. A reminder to those Russian and Chinese guns to get their aim right, not that they'd ever had trouble. It was never supposed to be a combat base, just a checkmark on a map to run patrols from, although six months into Dusty's tour every officer and newspaper was calling it the linchpin of the northern front. All they had was sandbags, Claymores, and three layers of German razor wire. Every week the vats of shit would get burnt off with diesel, blending with the smoke from the burning trees, the burning wreckage of a fuel plane on the airstrip, the burning grass. The .50 calibers were seven miles out, dug so deep the bombers couldn't deracinate them. No ground routes open, just the deathtrap airstrip for relief. Everyone knew how many battalions were in the forest around them, eight to their one. And everyone knew a ground assault was inevitable, factual, and they were waiting for it. Four months waiting in flimsy half-covered bunkers with your asshole squeezed tight to hold off the run to the latrine.

The trail is a slick cut, half-healed with mud. Slender white trunks and then the trees close over. The mahout slices the branches like they're celery, but still Dusty's catching them in the face: twigs and skittering brown leaves and sudden masses of thick spider silk, juiced with bug guts, some devious black maker with demon horns sprouting from its abdomen vanishing into the air, or just his shirt. The lizard's skin prickles his ankles with those fine, wasted quills. Water dumps down from leafy bowers. The mahout is silent except to chirrup orders at the beast. Once, when it shoulders into a sharp piece of deadfall, he moans sympathetically to it. He pats its neck. Once, when a trunk has fallen crosswise over the path, too low to duck under, too tall to step over, he smacks at the wood until the lizard seizes it in its jaws and tears it down to the ground like a party streamer. Dusty's seen all this before. He's paid to see it.

There were rumours of MIAs fighting for the other side. POWs eating their own bowels in tiger cages. Rumours that the enemy would chain themselves to their machine guns and melt hands off on red-hot muzzles, that they'd drug themselves into schizophrenic fugues and lie in spiderholes for weeks until someone walked into their crosshairs. Rumours of trails cut deep into valleys, wide enough for trucks. Rumours of hip-deep piles of lizard shit. Rumours of trained flyers the size of B52s sweeping the fringes of the DMZ, dive-bombing helicopters into the ground. Rumours of the mist. Of motionless, shark-toothed lizards. The soft hoots of their riders. On the trail ahead, Dusty detects his nineteen-year-old self, helmet and a flak jacket with a calendar countdown inked white on the back, creeping in the mulch, bowels loose, neck ant-bitten, feet rotten, forsaken. But it never came for him.

They wade through murky streams with sunlight filtering down to flashing, fleeing minnows. The trees vault overhead in a sacrosanct filigree. They pass over deadfall like busted station wagons. They arrive at a small pit. A sinkhole, Dusty guesses.

"Trap," says the mahout. "Hundred years old."

The trail here spiders, eight-legged, off into the forest. Ancient trails, made by ancient game, stalked by these predators for a million years. How a man carrying a weapon ever looked at this demon and believed he could subjugate it. That it was even capable of submission. Rotten-skin stink; evil older than God in its pupils. Thousands of armed men crushed and torn apart. This beast sprang straight from the pit. The mahout's lived in this village his whole life. Of course, Dusty doesn't say. They were here together. The lizard, too, miserable with its weeping orange eye. That pit would never have been big enough to hold it.

East of the temple there'd been a Special Forces base on Hill 775, a proper base with real defenses, real bunkers under six feet of concrete, twenty-four men. When the attack came they didn't recognize the sound of the T-34s because no one knew the enemy had T-34s. Their air vents and gun slits were likewise filled with shit that shouldn't have been: satchel charges, Bangalore torpedoes, napalm. Six survivors ran overnight through ten miles of jungle to the temple base. Everyone knew what it meant: the pit, and everything in it, had come for them.

At the temple, the lizard clanks and bows and Dusty slides down onto a collapsing stone wall. The mahout shackles the lizard's ankles and lights a cigarette. He looks off the escarpment, across the wetlands. The village is visible, as are the meagre herds.

Dusty climbs, sun-hazed, up the temple steps. The heat intensifies with each. The base is on the far side. His tiny plastic AK bangs his slick ribs. The temple was built for gods or tourists, its stones black and lurched with time's warp. Each step's haul is a memento mori: tall as his knee, barely a toehold to lever to the next. Seven-headed cobras guard the ascent. Two last frangipani trunks, with one branch left blooming between them after all these centuries. At the top, where the rock of the mount is carved in relics, and the holy spring tinkles gently in the sanctuary, he looks back.

After Hill 775 the shelling stopped. Patrols came back to report the jungle was empty. Not a tripwire or a sniper. The ground assault never came. On a clear day, Dusty walked across the tarmac with his duffel. Heard nothing but the grumble of tended engines.

The light's always the same, every memory and every day, colours brilliant and sick. Down there in the distance, the lizard is small. It shakes its head and flings out its tail, and its jaws gape to roar. But it is silent, and its maw, from way up here, is toothless.

Ryan & Irene,
Irene & Ryan

The dream is its own reality, so I can't be sure I'm awake until I walk into the office at eleven fifteen and see who's at reception. My office in the dream—in all the dreams—is the same as my office in life. Sunny, concrete, perfume lifted and dispelled by air conditioning. In the dream the receptionist is a girl who stopped speaking to me in middle school. This morning I am three hours late. I am unshowered, wearing a suit because nothing else was clean. No one wears suits here, not even Moe. But when the elevator doors open it's just an intern sitting behind the desk, so I know I'm awake. Everything is real.

"Morning, Mad," says the intern, smiling.

I frown past her to Vivian, my assistant, who waits like a meerkat in the bullpen. Maybe she stood there all morning, gazing at the elevator doors. No one else glances up from their screens. Coffees are sipped. Keyboards chitter.

Viv slides open my office door for me and says, "I moved Irene back to two."

"What did you tell her?"

"That the lawyers were running long. This is nice."

"Good." I put my purse on my desk.

"Balmain?"

"What?"

"Is it Balmain?"

I look down at my lapels. "Is it?"

"Yes, it is," she says.

Moe made me hire a personal shopper once. The woman tested me—dozens of Freudian slides—then presented, over a series of days, a stream of folded garments in white, or sometimes black and occasionally grey, saying that before I even considered another piece I should always meditate on *votre look*. She gave me a piece of black leather with words stamped in serif: *Surgeon. Sensei. Colonist.* I left her bill, which was insane, on Moe's desk.

"What about Tender?" I say.

"Told him you were putting out fires with Irene."

"Did you book the call with Gulf?"

"They suggested Wednesday ten or Thursday four."

"Wednesday, I guess."

Viv cocks her head. "So you're planning on coming in on time tomorrow then?" Her glossy bangs, cut straight and heavy, give her the appearance of a precocious twelve-year-old, always mocking me from within her immaculate ensemble. *Votre look: Aristocrat. Company man. Queen of the Detention Hall.*

"Shut up," I say.

"Rough night?" Viv is also too interested in personal things, mine and the clients' both. She is excellent, for a twenty-five-year-old, but still she is twenty-five. The entire office is twenty-five, except for Moe and me, and the nineteen-year-olds.

"It was fine," I say. I was dealing with the lawyers and publicists about Irene's ex, but that's not why I slept so late. The dream runs in tandem harness with reality, but it is separate and unique. It's hard to twist out of. In one night I can wake up a dozen times, still deep in it. Time fogs like it's long gone already. Last night in the dream I came to work, then went home and worked. I came to work, then went home and worked. You see why I have trouble telling everything apart.

"What did you tell everyone?" I ask.

"That you were out with a potential client."

"A client."

"Yeah, like, Rihanna."

"Rihanna?"

"I didn't." It disgusts her that I don't understand her jokes. "Obviously I did not. Do you want a coffee?"

I pause, blank. "Do you want one?"

"Sure," she sighs.

"Can you get food, too?" I dig a card out of the purse that woman bought me. "And whatever you're having."

Viv leaves the door open. I unfold my computer. Since closing it at three a.m. I've received another hundred emails, which puts me at twelve hundred unread. I've left so many fires to burn while dealing with Irene's ex. The email from Irene is titled *thank you* and it says, *everything feels so much better already, see you at 2.* I hope that means that she'll show up to our meeting unweeping. Although maybe it'll be just as well to give Tom, her new tour manager, a holistic picture.

"Here you go, Mad," says the mail guy. The package is white plastic ribbed in black electrical tape.

I don't look up because he is too attractive. Tattooed, narrow. I grab the package from the edge of my desk after he turns away, saw it open with my car keys. A handheld audio recorder. Some little band wanting attention. Or the lawyers? I press play.

A high whine.

They told me the glass walls fractured and crashed to the floor, but the fern beside my desk was unruffled.

In the dream, I'm skinning a kiwi on my patio. The valley below is emptied of houses, streets. The leaves on everything are primordial. I admire what the light does, gilding them. I'm unstructured in silk robe, slick hair. Irene and her ex confer in my kitchen, shrieking celery in the juicer.

Together in the same room, hands touching and re-touching in the coral-reef current between them, they make each other more beautiful. Irene's always hanging back like she's been strung from the ceiling. Grey skin, ashy hair. His name is Ryan. She has a tendency, in public, to speak inaudibly, but her laugh is huge and braying because she was raised with good brothers. Beside her, Ryan's alive: long, wall-scaling arms. He's pixie-faced, sparkle-eyed, currently wearing a moustache that would be unremarkable on a uniformed park ranger. He'd be an insolent waiter.

Irene is crying, her mascara a watercolour blackwash across her cheekbones. She says, "Leave, please. Look." Then to me: "I'm sorry. This is your house."

"Don't worry," I cross my arms over my breasts.

"I'm so embarrassed," she says. I guess they've been in my spare room all night. He would've come in through a window. There's no question the two of them were fucking like cats while I was an absurd lump, sleeping with my hand on my phone under the pillow, irradiated.

"Please just go," Irene says, and covers her face.

Ryan looks to me. I shake my head and shrug. I've never actually met him. She's my client. I've heard everything. I know in reality we've taken out a restraining order against him, but things are allowed to be different here. Some of the pain could be stripped from them, maybe.

"I'll go," I say. "Take your time. Call me if you need anything."

I pick up my car keys. My feet are bare. In the garage it's not the Audi, it's my old shitty Jeep, and my dog is waiting in it, though she won't look at me. We go to the beach and she swims into the ocean and keeps swimming. She doesn't come back.

White curtains and the tops of trees twitch outside the window. I will my body to move but it won't. A doctor comes in. My arms are swaddled like infants, the left one stopping six inches short.

"What's wrong?" I ask.

"Do you feel any pain?"

"I don't think so," I say.

"We cleaned up the forearm. We're waiting to see about the other one."

"The other one?"

"We'll see, but we're fairly sure it'll be fine."

"Where's my phone?" I ask.

"I have no idea," she says. "Did she have a phone?"

Moe is standing in the door. He's gleaming with sweat. It's droppletting the front of his beautiful white shirt. He's fat and handsome. When he hired me he promised he'd never interfere with my clients, that I'd take my twenty percent and he was just happy to have my name around. The man never shuts up or stops laughing. He doesn't come into the room. He gawks.

"Do you have my phone?" I ask.

He moans. He leaves.

The bandages are yellowed, yellowing. I can't move my arms, but then I can. One swings like a construction crane. It hits some tubing that's attached to me, and I draw it back in across my chest.

Moe comes back. He says, "Holy shit, Mad. Vivian's looking for it. But I guarantee you it melted with the rest of everything on your desk. It's probably lodged in the fucking ceiling right now."

"I'm really behind, Moe," I confess. I've been wanting to say it for months, but immediately I want to unsay it.

He doesn't acknowledge me. He comes to the bed and looks at my left bandage. "Do you remember what the package said? The police want to talk to you about that. Is she up for that?" He looks for the doctor, but she walked out ages ago.

"Everything got away from me," I say. Heat leaks from the sides of my eyes. I shouldn't admit it. But I'm so relieved to tell him. There's nothing he can do. My throat closes up. My clients are all angry. Everyone but Irene. I could lose Tender, I could lose Bishop Weyland. I wouldn't blame them.

"Mad," he says. "Madeleine."

I open my eyes. "Listen. What is going on here? Is Irene okay?"

"Irene?" Moe says. "Jesus, forget her melodrama for a second."

"Was there some kind of car accident or something?"
I ask.

"What? No," Moe says. He sits down in the chair beside
me. He's staring at my chest, or my arms crossed vampir-
ically over it. He's hot and red and his face has a fixedness
to it that is becoming terrifying. I don't recognize his fea-
tures in this shape. "Holy shit," he says, again.

Irene refuses to bring me to her favourite bar for meetings,
and she also refuses to come into the office because there
have been times, yes, when we've ordered in lunch, and
dinner, and another dinner. I don't always know when to
stop. That was when we were first getting set up, though,
and I was untangling the mess Poseidon had made. Crew,
accounting, booking agents. A real tour manager. Now
we meet at this bar she hates, the one with expensive artis-
anal cocktails that she thinks will motivate me to wrap up
quickly. She orders gin, I order soda. The server is wearing
a vintage tuxedo and a tiny moustache. Of course the place
has no name. Moe's friend Marcus owns it and calls it Bar
No Name. Irene will wither under any glint of attention.
At first people just see her jawline, her poltergeist figure,
the negative oxygen suck of her strikingness, but then
there's the spread of recognition. This is not the kind of
place where anyone will approach her, though the server
is embarrassingly familiar. He brings us a plate of olives,
"Viz our compliments," he says.

"He's faking that accent," Irene says. "He can't make
up his mind between French and German."

"Swiss?" I say. I open my laptop. I don't know, I avoid
travelling too much. All my clients know I won't tour with
them. It's part of the deal. I'm supposed to be worth it.

My email chimes, and Irene, leaning back into the white leather, wreathed in waxy palm fronds, smiles. No one's supposed to work explicitly anymore, I know. Viv has told me repeatedly that looking at my phone is not socially okay.

"Gulf has some names for the new bio."

"Okay," she says.

"They have someone to shoot the interview. Turn the footage into teasers."

"Who do they want to write it?"

"No one I recognized. Some kid from London? Let me look." I click around, searching for the conversation.

"Have you heard from Ryan?" This is what she actually wants to talk about.

"I haven't. Has he been—" I stare into my silver light.

"No." She twists her gin, lifts it to cradle near her heart.

I click through labels and tabs. What is the woman who does international's name? Maude. Meghan. Meagan. I type *bio* in the search box and two thousand conversations come up.

"He's never actually left me alone before."

"It's a restraining order."

Finally, I'd called the police. The night he wouldn't leave her foyer, the door buzzing constantly, the magazine photographer—nineteen years old mentally if not physiologically—giggling and peering down through the front window to the stoop where he stood, Allison the publicist staring at me with increasing heat, Irene handing me her phone and retreating to the bathroom to sob, then coming back smiling weakly and shivering. I read his endless, contorting scroll: *You talentless, starfucking piece of shit. You've fucked me over do your own vapid soul for the last time. Don't you dare contact me again you*

*fucking bitch. Your all I want. We're conjoined I'm abso-
lutely fucked inside. Please. One more chance.* She curled
like a greyhound on the couch. I looked outside: he stood
in the street with his chin lifted. The police came up to
take our statements. Allison hissed, smiling, into my ear:
"This is so bad."

The sun on Irene is green-gold through the leaves. Her
freckles look like worry scattered under deep-socketed,
apologetic eyes. She could be a sickish art-gallery clerk,
undiagnosable without health care; or some court sorcer-
ess tasked with sitting awake all night to keep the cats and
night hags off a happier woman's baby. I love Irene. It's a
side effect of looking at her.

"He's not stupid," she says. "He's batshit, but." Then
weeping again. Not sobbing, just glossy-eyed. I know the
overview: five years spiralling around him and she got
three albums out of it, including the one that broke her.
Even before she fired the predator of a manager she'd
started with, there was a cold war for her talent: I only won
because she wanted me. Me, because everyone knows what
I've done for Tender. We've only had each other since
Christmas, but she still hasn't signed my contract. I never
forget I'm still on trial. My job is to spin her talent into
money, but no one else ever called the cops.

"You gave him every opportunity," I say.

"I just—I don't know how to. Who else can I tell about
this remix, you know?" She swirls a hand in the air. Bruce
Springsteen or a coyote yips over the speakers.

I grimace. The server, for one, would happily listen to
her thoughts, as would any number of the ostentatiously
disinterested people in this bar. But this is the problem.
Fame corrodes everything.

"I know, I don't mean to be. It's just what's in my head. You're not. Creatively, it was an important—"

"I understand, Irene."

"It's just withdrawal. He was always going to—" She inhales. She sips. Her eyes skitter across the room behind me. "I guess it's all the other women, now."

"Withdrawal," I repeat.

"If I just think of myself as an addict," she says.

"Is there—" I don't know what to say. "Does that help?"

She has calmed. She is wrapped in her black kaftan. Her gin dampens her knee. "I wish I could warn them. But I'd seem crazy, wouldn't I?"

I turn back to my emails. "Mavis," I mutter. The list of music writers appears.

"What if he's all I have to write about?" she says.

I don't answer her. I have no answer.

In the dream, when he comes through the window I'm there this time. He's not embarrassed to find me.

"Can I help you?" I say. He locks the window after sliding it closed. A spider the size of my hand skitters across the glass and disappears.

He has a scar under one eye and premature crow's feet from years spent in weather. Stringy biceps. He's always so flushed, dry, burnt up. The light is yellow from the hall. I meet his eyes and then can't. My watch beeps. It's green velcro, a gift from my father when I was in junior high. I'm in a full sweat like back then. Hormones.

I try again. "Can I get you anything?"

His hands are still, like they want nothing, but his body is vibrating. I can tell because we're standing so close. If I could just be of some use to him. His mother died last year. Irene told me. Irene told me everything evil about him. The good was untranslatable. A separate stream. He has one hand on my sternum. There's a gorge open there that I'd welcome him into. I don't recognize this room. It's his, I guess. He has a whole wing of my house and this is the first time I've been into it. He kisses me with his eyes open so that he can watch Irene where she sits in an armchair in the corner by an armoire, holding her throat and sobbing so hard she's coughing, choking, pulling at a pendant around her neck until the cheap metal chain breaks.

I lie, mummified. I have questions. Who would the hospital have called if I hadn't been at work? If Viv and Moe and the hot mailman hadn't known my name and insurance details? I keep a card in my wallet with a few names blacked out: my ex-husband who remarried, a friend who lives in New York, for a while my trainer at the gym, who would text me in a friendly way that I strained into reading as flirtation. But I was paying my trainer, which meant we probably each had a different understanding of the situation, and I was too embarrassed to tell him his name was on that card, so eventually I blacked him out, too.

The cops come and go. Moe says I have to make a statement for the press release. I say, "I look forward to starting my new bionic life." Allison rolls her eyes but says that she can work with it. I don't ask if they know who sent the package, and no one volunteers any ideas.

The sharpie did not do a perfect job. A nurse walks me down the hall to the pay phone and dials the number I read through the ink. My ex-husband is newlywed. There's no mirror in my washroom, so I assume I now look demonic.

Charred, scarred. We talk about his honeymoon in French Polynesia. We had planned to go to Tahiti on our fifteenth anniversary, but we only made it to twelve. He invited me to his wedding, but I declined on the grounds I'd never made myself very likable to his friends. "What else is new?" I say.

"Not much. Dog's good. She's doing that tongue thing again."

"Send me a picture."

"Sure."

"Oh, actually, you can't. My phone blew up."

"Like exploded?" He's amiable. He's driving home to his wife.

"I'm in the hospital," I say.

"Seriously?"

"It was on the news."

"What was on the news?"

"A mail bomb blew my hand off."

"Holy god, Mads," he laughs.

"Will you come visit?"

"You're kidding, right?" he says. I remember that he moved with the dog to Denver two years ago.

"No?" I say. "The nurse had to give me a special pillow to hold the phone."

"Wait."

"I look super cool right now."

"Wait," he squawks. "You're not kidding?"

He probably won't come.

There's less blood than I would've thought. The pain is mostly a frightening lack of pressure, a carsick lightness that wakes me up over and over again. My head jerks up, drifts down, jerks up. The nurses keep it sedated. Irene has not come.

Irene told me about how Ryan, three years into their relationship, was summoned by a dying hairdresser, who bought him a plane ticket to visit her deathbed. Just a hook-up, he'd said. Why would this dying woman want to see him? He didn't know. He spent six months evading the trip. The dying woman got angry, accused him of using the ticket for something else and not telling her. Coward. When he finally went, he booked the trip over Irene's birthday. "What's wrong with you?" he'd said. "She's *dying*, Irene."

I have options as to prosthetics. If I spend the money, I can have one that looks like Apple made it. Pellucid, streamlined. An improvement on the hand. I've always had short, ugly nails. Who needs the weakest digits, besides to apply under-eye cream? I'll be able to type and percolate coffee, do some light yoga. No inversions, obviously. Viv shows me my phone: screen cracked, cover blown off the back. She sits beside me and I dictate: tour support for Europe, the launch timeline, ad buys. I was never that into yoga, though. There is one vase of tropical flowers, and fifty-three more at the office. The intern at reception was lost in them so they had to start spreading them out, two per desk. I can't decide: either Viv is exaggerating the number to make me feel beloved, or everyone in the office is enjoying the swell of good feeling while I lie here with one bunch of daylilies and alpinia. Irene has not come. The pain medication makes it easy to weep constantly, weakly, about how everything is happening without me now.

"Has Irene called?" I ask again.

"No," says Viv, her eyes sliding away and back to the screen.

"But she knows."

"I emailed her. We spoke on the phone."

It's been four days.

"She's probably with Ryan," I say, and Viv's eyebrows twitch up, though she keeps typing. "They've probably run off to Morocco together."

"Ha," says Viv. She treats most things I say as a joke.

"Call her again."

"Sure," she says, in the way that means she'll forget until I ask again. She sighs. "I'll never understand women like that."

I raise my left bandage to my mouth. It smells starchy, unclean. Old upholstery, a gelatin factory. The pain, sometimes, is just the need to crack my knuckles.

Onstage at the Belvedere, Irene is her own high priestess. Her hair shrouds her as she fiddles with pedals and murmurs into the mic. I stand sidestage behind the guitar tech as he consults the set list by penlight and ignores me. I'm in situ so rarely that I'm often mistaken for someone's girlfriend, but after a week of production rehearsals for the North American run—I brought my laptop from the office, cleared some pizza boxes from a closet—half the crew can at least recognize me, though it's still only the tour manager, Tom, who'll speak to me. Tour managers are a favoured breed. *Votre look: Dive bartender. Super-mom. Warzone logistician.* Tom passes a rummy plastic cup and I hold onto it. Beside me, Tender, looking not long for this world, stands like a stork on one foot and sucks back his vodka.

"She is so beloved," he says, leaning into me. We can't see the audience, but they're shrieking like a bat colony. His mouth touches my ear, on purpose. I shiver. Tender's habits hope for an early death. He's painted his face paler, his bony shoulders and bare ribs exposed by the night-blue silk shirt eternally falling off him. I've managed him for twelve years and he's made three albums for every one he's let me release. He's too big to bill as support for Irene, but he'd begged—*I am begging you*—so we'd let it leak he would. Hometown kick-off to the world tour, Irene could've filled a stadium, but we gave away the tickets to this little one: eight hundred humans in a time machine with velvet curtains winging the proscenium, living simultaneously in this moment and the one three years ago when this song was playing on the radio and everyone who heard it knew they'd survive.

I turn away from the meet-and-greet after the show: nearing that line-up of sweating and trembling is too much. Tom cuts and aligns fans like a border collie or a coke dealer. I abandon my untouched rum on a console worth more than my car and retreat upstairs to the green room, where it's mostly Tender's locals: thin limbs and pretty faces I only vaguely recognize line the tiny room's couches like a panel of judges. Viv is in there with an aloof smirk. Good for her. Except she beckons me in, and Tender passes me another plastic cup and I wait for someone to say something I can speak to: streaming royalties, equipment carnets. But the conversation is all MDMA and rent.

Irene comes in, eyes glassed, hair dried to salted twine. The room and Tender wrap around her and she goes loose like he's snagged her by the nape. His talent's always been making you yearn like an exile. I almost put a hand out between them, but am too shocked by my jealousy. She pushes him away instantly: "God. I'll cry. Please, Nick." She shakes her head, smiling and apologizing, and fades back out of the room, which wilts after her. Viv raises an eyebrow at me.

I guard Irene's door for two minutes, then tap it myself. "Irene?"

"Who are they?" she says. A dozen pine-scented tea lights burn a witchy forest fire. Her eyes are blacked like a falcon's. "Like, I don't really know any of those people."

"Do you mean names?" I say. "I can ask."

"No. I don't care. I'd rather hang out with Tom and Gonzalo, but they're busy loading up my stupid shit."

"Is it—" I try to guess. "The show was unbelievable."

"Jesus. What does that mean?"

I blank my face. I wait. I say, humanely, "You just seem upset."

"Do I? Do you want to be more condescending about it?"

I surrender my palms.

She rattles the ice in a cup. "Just tell me where my friends are. Why weren't my friends in that room?"

I saw the guest list. I can't say I know what friends she's talking about. She didn't invite any. She takes a lighter from her pocket and lights more candles.

"No one's here," she mutters.

"None of your friends," I repeat, soft.

"They all left me," she says. She clicks the lighter. She hooks a thumb through a necklace; the long one with a tine of antler dangling from it. She grinds the tip of it into the heel of her hand. "They all got sick of it. It was too boring, I guess, when he was all I ever talked about."

"That's a beautiful necklace," I say.

Her eyes dart up. She lifts it. "Can you take it?"

"Um—"

"I promised myself I'd give it to the first person who complimented it."

"No, that's—"

"I know it's a little woodsy for you." She narrows her eyes at my dress, which makes me look like an aesthetician from the blizzarding steppe. "But give it away, whatever. I can't keep it. It's cursed."

The antler, copper-wound, is warm in my hand. I do not want to put the chain around my neck. Irene crying and choking in that armchair while he kissed me. It's easy to understand why she's allowed him to return so many times. Forgiveness is a grace.

"Sorry," she says. "I'm sorry."

"Irene, you know you can't offend me," I say. I would've held her, if she'd looked up. "Whatever you need."

I find Tom closing out with the merch guy. "Bring her some pizza," I tell him. "And blow out those candles."

Out on the floor under the house lights, the venue staff sweep plastic cups and confetti as the crew disassembles the rig. I drop the antler. It'll find its own in the trash.

In the dream, Ryan sweats the bed to soaking. In his wing, words are tamped down with crypt dust and incense. It's impossible to speak. I visit him there, dress, and leave, knowing myself less and less. "I didn't send a fucking bomb," he says. "That's insane." He lies, liar. He deletes truth like weather deletes history, imperfectly. He says Irene has victimized herself, twisted everything her way. She treats all her friends, family, past lovers the same. He is human and fallible. He could say things about her, but he won't. Time fogs like it's long gone already. I have

61

both hands, all my fingers flex elegantly. I call Irene, over and over, but she doesn't answer. "She pretended she was going to kill herself," he confesses. "She wrote fake suicide letters. She manipulated me with her emotions." It's my house, so I watch another dozen women enter and exit, comforting him. They see each other but stay silent. Their shoulders brush in the foyer as they take off their shoes, wrap their scarves. Please—I'd say, if they could hear me—don't delete yourselves.

I am still in hospital when the Bataclan happens. "They flipped the soundboard up and hid behind it," Tender reads, voice strange. He holds too tightly to my good arm, even though the burns are ugly, and in the end the doctor decided to take off two of its fingers.

Ed calls from Zurich, voice high. "We want to come home now," he says. Cancelling the rest of Bishop Weyland's continental grind will cost as much as recording their next LP, but they're only twenty. They have pimples and the whites of their eyes are bright.

"I know you do," I say. "Give me a few hours."

Viv, on my other side, says, "Did you read about the merch guy? His girlfriend was all over social media trying to find out if he was okay. But there was this other woman who was at the show, giving him mouth-to-mouth. He died in her arms. And they're both going, 'He was the love of my life.' Word for word." She shakes her head. "Can you imagine finding out that way?"

"I don't think you're even aware of what you're saying," says Tender. "Or at least I hope you're not."

Viv pauses a half-second too long. Her voice is a crystal ting of apology: "Yes, you're right."

Tender shakes his head. "You know you have to actually try to care. It takes effort."

"Oh, definitely," says Viv demurely.

"Jesus. There's nothing more callous than a twenty-eight-year-old woman."

"Maybe just women in general," Viv suggests. "You would know."

"Please stop," I say. "Nick. Just go, for a little bit. Both of you."

This morning I saw my new reflection. They've been looking at me this whole time and didn't tell me. How is it possible that I missed it? Hyper-sensitive, that's what makes me good at this job. Perfectly attuned, no boundaries between their needs and mine. I'm part of them, until I'm not. I need to text Jonathan, Bishop Weyland's tour manager, and tell him to make Ed eat something, sleep a bit, before I talk to him again and convince him they're fine, they can keep going. But I can't text anyone. Ryan's bomb took a hand and a half. I have three fingers, three limbs.

Irene stands in my door. She looks like a vow of poverty. Soft-soled, tattered. Now I know what disturbs my visitors, but I don't turn my face away from her. She is weeping, but she is always weeping. What kind of person takes another's suffering as an attack? She keeps the rope she noosed to hang herself with coiled on a bookshelf in her living room. I've seen it. It could suit an aesthetic: *Sailor. Convict. Casualty.*

"Can we pretend that I came right away?" she says.

"Come here," I say, and she hugs me, smells the dead horse of me, the black dust on me. She lifts a hip and slips onto the bed with me. She is a bandage.

"They arrested him," she says into my neck, under my ear. "He sent one to the lawyers. They caught it right away."

"I know," I tell her.

"He never sent one to me." Her tiny voice.

"I'm sorry," I say. I lift my hand to touch her hair, then lower the bandaged stump soundlessly.

She is suffering because she could be in Morocco with him. Panama. He's tried to kill for her, which makes her more special to him than the others. We are conjoined, he'd tell her. Forgiveness is the temptation she's damned to. Eighty-nine people shot dead in a concert hall. Violence scales more effortlessly than art. We're all going to die one day. Her thumb rubs smooth the furrow in my brow. Her body holds emotion like smoke in a barricaded room. I hold her body. I protect it with my own.

Thanatos

This view, I make explicit to the child, has shattered the unity through which I had thought I could extend my sovereignty to the bodies of my past. What's the good of mutilation? What I wanted: a guarantee. I'm not the pigeon on Tesla's windowsill. The child is in the kitchen, sitting on the tile, unscrewing caps from liquor bottles. Bottles that people have given me that I have not given away again. People no longer want to give me things. The child is inhaling the fumes from each open neck, recoiling, recapping. She's a neat child. She rarely speaks to me. Last night she wailed and I asked her, "What's wrong? What's the matter?"

"What if he doesn't come?" she cried, pulling at her hair, snotting green.

We've been waiting here for a week. The *New Yorker* described this condo, which has two bedrooms, as austere. Other gifts: my *TIME* cover, my *Forbes* cover, my *Glamour* cover, framed. The child crunched the glass out of them when she was curled in the hall closet and cut herself, and we decided together the cut was superable and that we would not exit the condo to consult a doctor. I sewed her up.

I explained my celibacy several times to him, but Henry Kissinger kept setting me up on dates. The day before I was barred from owning or operating a laboratory, and our valuation went from six billion to zero, he and the board of directors threw me a surprise birthday party. Domination is fixed in rituals. I am trying to move through history. They mourned my youth excessively. "Our wunderkind," Henry Kissinger assured the employees, "Is still a wonder." "She'll be needing treatment herself, soon! Ha ha!" said Admiral Lee. The stigmata of their past errors, deviations, faulty calculations, is engraved in their bodies. When I was nine I built a time machine.

We are running out of food a little but the child doesn't eat anyway.

A pigeon is at the windowsill in the kitchen. Tesla described his beloved as purest white with silver-tipped wings: the most beautiful pigeon in the world. This pigeon is mauve with pink talons and doesn't flinch when I seize her. A tiny cylinder contains a note:

> *Charlotte,*
>
> *This is a time when Thanatos needs to rebuild confidence. You are abandoning your life's work. You need to make a decision before the damage you're doing becomes irreparable.*
>
> *Henry Kissinger.*

I drop the note over the windowsill. It drifts three storeys and settles in the hibiscus. The purple pigeon chuckles off. What I wanted: a new episode in subjugation. Not this spectacle of a struggle. The FDA doesn't believe me, or the NIH or the SEC. They want me to skin my science. So does the entire pharmaceutical industry, every plastic surgeon, every venture capitalist who turned his libertarian nose up, every precious journalist. There is no common space between us. At seventeen, a sophomore at Harvard, I incised the flanks of a twelve-month-old mouse and a two-month-old mouse and I sewed their skins together so their capillaries enmeshed, and their cerebrovascular architecture remodelled and increased in volume by eighty-seven percent and their newborn neuron populations enhanced by ninety-two percent and when I sewed Lorraine Armster-Prickett to a fifteen-year-old girl who'd lost her hands to a barrel bomb in the Siege of Hama, yes, the hair was silkier and the mind sharper and the skin more elastic after five weeks unconscious on a cushioned dais. And naturally, five weeks on an IV drip has all the hormetic benefits of calorie restriction, that is, hippocampal neurogenesis and modulated physiological senescence and satisfying weight loss, though some of the weight is muscle mass, it's true. Lorraine woke up delighted to be weak as a petal.

After he accepted my invitation to chair the board, Henry Kissinger advised me to stop recruiting my youthful parabionts from refugee camps. "You will be perceived as experimenting on them," he said. "Use Americans."

"No," I said. Force, flagging, inflicts torments and mortifications in the name of morality. Lorraine paid five hundred thousand US dollars to Amira, and seventy-five to me. I paid Duc, my lab technician, and the lab's landlord, and the lawyers. The scar runs from armpit to hip. One of them lies on her belly, the other lies on her back. They entwine, armpit to armpit, hip to hip. Thirteen years have passed and the waitlist has become incalculable. Amira's forearms taper to her tiny wrists and when she sleeps she crosses them over her chest like an ancient queen.

"There are poor Americans," Henry Kissinger insisted. "Everyone has a housekeeper."

"No," I told him.

The child is reading the newspaper. It's fine if there's no food; all I drink is vegetable juice. The waitlist elongated because I had a mirror list for individuals falling off the ledge of dementia. But the youthful parabiont must still be paid— it's not for charity they're inheriting some fifty-year-old memory, or unpopular opinion on natural-gas regulation. I hired staff. More lawyers. I incorporated Thanatos. I doubled the cost of treatment. It's easy to woo board members when the studies are patient-funded. The directors have signed exe-cution orders, captained aircraft carriers, declared war. One, Clive, is a cardiac surgeon. I am truly sorry for the fact that he tried to kill himself. The last date Henry Kissinger sched-uled: a man who explained the fluid mechanics of liberty in his private floating city, then-imaginary. He ordered horse tartar and an IPA. "History should be a curative science," I snapped, standing up. We had both worn black turtlenecks.

The child is picking at her stitches. This is the interstice. This is a non-place. Yes, I have de-automated my body and achieved a granularity of attention in this period of removal. Anyway, nothing in me is stable enough that I can recognize myself. I have no money, but all of my cruelty is intact. By the end I couldn't participate in the intake interviews. I left it to Duc. They'd ask, "Can you target the skin around my eyes? What about my hymen? Get it down to a vice. À la carte? So how long until I have to re-up? My staff can't function for that long. I'll fund you. I'll skip the list. From now on."

The youthful don't ask questions. Their mothers don't. I bring the accountant with me. We sit in the hotel lobby and drink tea. They say, "There were ten thousand men missing and four thousand bodies. My biggest fear is that our lives were a failure. A neighbour came and suggested we get fire-wood. She can't take care of a husband like this. She is thirteen. She doesn't sleep. He might be alive, he might be dead."

The child is screaming. I walk around until I find her at the top of the stairs. Something is broken at the bottom of them, but I don't recognize it.

One day Tesla's beloved flew into his hotel room with starlight shining from her eyes and told him that death would soon be elective. Then she died in his arms and he knew his life's work was over.

When I was nine I used the time machine to go into the future and meet myself. I stole my mother's wallet and took a bus from Houston to Palo Alto. In the future I told security my name was Charlotte Giang and they led me upstairs. I was waiting. I offered myself a vegetable juice. "Listen," I said. I was smiling, gentle wisps of hair haloing my fat, happy face. "You don't have to worry, you'll fall in love on December 31, 2018."

It is December 31, 2018. I vowed myself to celibacy before I lost my virginity to chance. Tesla was a virgin, but he invented the death ray. After my birthday party ended at five p.m., when my employees went home, I cried for two hours in my favourite conference room, which is when I noticed the child also weeping in the same conference room. Either my nine-year-old self or my thirty-nine-year old self had deposited her there. That night, Duc called and told me the SEC and the FDA and the NIH had imposed sanctions against me. Not against Thanatos. Not against the teleological essence of the work. Against me. You have to understand that this is not psychology. It's madness' own monologue about reason.

"What if," says the child, clinging wetly to my neck, hiding her face from the thing at the bottom of the stairs, "When he comes he doesn't like us?"

"He'll like us," I say.

"What if he just goes away again?"

"Listen," I say. "You don't have to worry."

"But I AM worried."

"It wouldn't matter," I say.

"Yes it WOULD."

"Why do you say that?"

"BECAUSE THEN I'M ALL ALONE."

"But I'm right here."

"YOU DON'T COUNT! YOU NEVER COUNTED!"

"Well," I say. "I think I do."

What I wanted: to prove that knowledge is not made for understanding; it is made for cutting. The child's wound runs up the arch of her foot, along her Achilles tendon. I dab it with antibiotic unguent. I admire my dainty stitches.

My doorbell makes the sound of a pigeon tapping on the glass. Amira and her mother spent the money fishing everyone they know out of Zaatari, but they left the rest. Henry Kissinger will make me fire my employees and myself. My self at the bottom of the stairs looks to be fifteen, but she's unrecognizable.

My doorbell makes the sound of a death ray.

My glowing future had glossy eyes as she cupped my face, "A pure, solid, and honest love is coming for you."

What is it I wanted?

The child is limping, scrambling, on two hands and one foot, towards the door.

The Emperor

While he was still married, Popov patrolled the mountain atop his great black gelding. The tack was all black leather, as were the boots. The uniforms were tailored and midnight blue. The administration, at the time, was hiring a lot of young women.

They sauntered root-buckled paths under the trees, in pairs or triads, alongside cyclists pumping to work and leashed dogs shocked cautious by their monstrous bodies. Only once in those years did he kick the gelding to full power—catapulting through branches, clawing rock and leafy loam with yellow talons, branches thrashing his helmet and shoulders, his cheek pressed to the hot throat, inhaling a sweet green foam of sweat and foliage—after a kid who'd hurled a broken bottle.

Popov took a leave to manage the funeral when his father died. The will required a swing band and three hundred guests. He called in a favour for the piano, which, once arrived, required a tuner. The will required the priest to speak French, and Popov paid one to come from an appropriate parish. His mother was repainting the house. He left Lucette, his wife, and went there to stay with her.

The night before the service, he drove his mother into the city. She bought him a green shirt to go with his eyes. She paid for dinner at a close, dark restaurant. She didn't ask about Lucette. They drank a bottle of wine and she said, "Have you ever dated a black woman?" She giggled. "What if a woman showed up at your door with a baby? With a six-year-old?"

"That wouldn't happen," he said.

"No, but if it did?" she murmured, gleeful.

At another table, a whippish blonde gazed past her date, slowly spinning her glass on the table.

"That woman keeps looking at you," said his mother.

Popov didn't glance over immediately, but when he did, the blonde was looking back. She was the kind who'd expect a lot of attention. Later, as he followed his mother out, he turned sideways between the cramped tables and met her eyes. The blonde quirked her lips at his crotch.

At home, Lucette was barely pregnant. She came out on the train for the service and kissed his mother on both cheeks, saying, "*Je suis désolée*," in her stumbled accent. She wept in the pew while he shook everyone's hand. It had all taken weeks; the body was long burnt. In the guest bed that night, Lucette mumbled under heavy covers, and he dressed and sat, drunk, in the mahogany dining room. He woke in sunlight and made coffee for his mother while Lucette coughed over the toilet.

After the kid on the mountain, la Directrice waved him into a conference room with three silvery administrators. "You're late, poodle, sit down." It was an accident, they had concluded. The journalists would be dealt with, the gelding sequestered. The young women la Directrice kept hiring were mostly assigned to answer calls from retail security and intimidate teens at the mall. Or else they'd liaise at high schools, where their hard vests and high ponytails gave them specific authority.

"Or you could do bicycles," la Directrice offered.

"Why not a clown school?" Popov said.

"In the summer there will be parades, at least," she said. "Or perhaps we will have another riot."

Once, Lucette had been sick and he'd gone to her apartment to feed her snake. The snake, like the rats it ate, was albino. He pincered the rodent's naked tail, rolled it between his thumb and forefingers. The rat twisted in the air as the snake's red eye opened.

The new uniform was a light and friendly blue. No glossy helmet or tall boots. He surveilled the boys in the corridors. He gave a presentation about pimps to the teachers on their professional development day. He stayed late one Wednesday and found ranks of students in dark tunics practicing parade drill on the football field. He lingered at the fence as three flagbearers led them down the yard lines. Their petty officer called an about turn in the end zone.

When asked, Popov said, "He was ready for it, he really chose his time. I have no regrets. We left nothing unsaid."

He did not see the gelding again.

He'd walk through the midnight park, where empty bottles were left beside the trashcans for the collectors' ease. Red and purple lanterns glowed in the trees, fire-eaters drizzled butane over their swabbed sticks. He kept an eye out. When the riots had first started, la Directrice had sent him with a black mask to join in the rock-throwing, but the militants had known him by his boots. Often, he would sit by himself on a bench under the branches while the lonely men walked through the crowded dark, mistaking him for one of themselves.

Lucette had mistaken him, once—back when she was working on the Main. He was sitting at a table with a visiting friend who kept insisting on how sensual the city's women were. "Sensual," he said, "Not necessarily more attractive, but, somehow more..." Lucette glanced once, and kept glancing from where she stood talking to a customer at the bar, but she did not come over to offer a dance. Popov understood the economics. He paid for a dance from another woman. He paid too much for each drink. His friend told a woman how much his watch had cost, and which hotel he was staying at. "I work in intelligence," he said.

When Lucette finally came over, Popov said, "Finally."

"Pardon?" she said in English. Her eyes narrowed at him.

"Great dance," he'd said, also in English.

She examined his tone, her spine stiff, then said, "Thank you," and walked away. Later, she told him she'd been unnerved by his handsomeness, and that she'd gone to the alley to smoke and apply lipstick. Popov's friend went briefly into a private room and came back complaining, wanting to go to a new club. Lucette touched Popov's arm as he was buying his coat back from the doorman.

He turned and she hugged him. "Come back at three," she said into his ear.

He patted her. Her hair clung in coarse strands to the damp skin of her back. At the next club, he found a slip of paper with her name and phone number in his pocket.

He didn't plan to return, but his friend became belligerent and embarrassing, and Popov's apartment was in that direction, and at three she was wearing jeans and flats, reading her phone under the marquee. The sidewalk was stained. Drunk students shouted. Her hair coiled down one lapel. She cocked a happy smile at him, as if it had been too long. They walked up the mountain together, under the trees. She'd lost the bird precision of her work heels. She was the kind who'd gain weight easily. She said, "Do you have a condom?"

"Of course I do," he said. "Don't you speak French?"

"No," she said. "I just moved here. I love this city." She grinned, mouth against his jacket. Her hands foraged his pockets. He caught her wrist, thinking of his wallet. "Let's fuck in the woods," she said.

"I don't think so," he said.

She laughed at him, her other hand on his crotch.

He didn't laugh.

"You're kidding," she said.

He let go of her wrist to catch her hand, but she pulled it back.

"What? Are you afraid of getting caught?" She laughed again, but her friendliness had chilled. She said nothing as they walked back down into the city.

At the first empty intersection she turned north. "It's been enchanting."

"I'll walk you home," he said. The light turned red. Nothing moved.

She shook her head, but allowed him to walk beside her.

At her door, she said: "I'm tired." Then, "I fuck enough in a bed."

The helicopters grated the dawn. The sky was white by the time he reached his own front step.

When she called him the next night she was friendly again. They drank five gins each on her balcony. She pulled back the flowery cover on her bed as she undressed herself. The sheets were gritty. "You dumped the whole forest in here?" he asked. She laughed. Her snake, thick as a thigh, was knotted in a tank on the floor. He didn't notice it till after, when she had her head burrowed into his wet armpit. "He's part of my act," she said.

They drank jars of water naked in her kitchen. He'd mouthed her makeup off and her eyelids were bald. She put her arms around him and placed her cheek between his shoulder blades.

"You're like coming home," he said, and she laughed so hard he pulled away.

"Do women let you get away with this?" she said. Yet she hadn't made him use the condom.

The street below was loud, and the sound of men hitting each other and a woman calling for them to stop woke them from half-sleep. He did not move from the sheets, but she went into the bathroom. When she came back, she writhed warmly against him.

"I'm a police officer," he said.

"I thought you said you were a spy," she said.

"That wasn't me," he said.

"Right," she said. "I forgot which asshole."

He saw her twice more. Then she had a fever. When he visited her, she was slouched on the edge of her mattress, as if she'd tried to greet him at the door.

"Come to my house," he said. "You're going to drown in this swamp. Come on."

"No," she said, then weakened.

His apartment was large and new in an old part of town. He put on fresh sheets. Every time she went to the bathroom to piss he'd hear her sobbing on the toilet. He called in sick to watch her sweat. She spent three days—first humid, then dryly listless—in his bed. She wouldn't say what was wrong. After the fever broke she spent the afternoon in a shallow salt bath. She covered her body if he looked at it.

She went to the clinic and came back humiliated. "You have to go see the doctor, too," she said. He bent his head in the waiting room. For months he handled his cock carefully, looked it over. Nothing ever manifested.

On the fourth night, she clung to him under the covers. "Could I at least suck on your dick a little?"

"I don't think so," he said.

She tightened into herself, invertebrate.

In the morning she got up to join him in the kitchen. She opened his fridge. He poured coffee. He said, "Who was it?"

She turned, barefoot on the tile, to look at him.

"Who gave it to you, I mean," he said.

"It was you," she said, slow, as if he were tricking her.

"Not necessarily," he said.

He did not understand her expression. She pulled a clawful of bleached hair by the roots from her scalp. If she had sobbed, he would not have seen her again. He had no tolerance for manipulation. But the hair drifted to the floor, and she picked it up and put it in the trash.

The year after that she got pregnant, and his father died, and he married her.

"She's so serious," his mother said to him in French when he brought her for dinner. "You are always dating such serious girls." Unarmed, Lucette looked to him across the table.

At that time, the black gelding was living in the stable with the others, exercised by paid attendants who cleaned its claws, stroked its beak.

At school, he spoke to the black-coat cadets about career paths. "Usually they want to be pilots," said the adult woman who commanded them. He wore his old uniform and showed pictures of himself mounted. He said, "There are many opportunities for specialization within the force."

A dozen of them sat at the small desks. One girl wore her hair crisped into gleaming plaits. Her cap lay flat beside her notebook as she doodled or took notes. She had three chevrons on each shoulder and wore a pin that said LALIBERTÉ.

"Officers are expected to use various levels of intervention to restore order and safety," he said, before they could ask about his gun.

Lucette's snake had red eyes and skin argyled ivory and gold. Only much later did he see the act she required it for, different from her usual work. This act happened at art galleries or after-parties where she wore her hair slicked to her skull. She'd thread a red feather needle straight through her cheek.

He asked to see the act, and she said he wouldn't like the audience. He asked to be invited to a performance, and she promised to ask the promoter. Three times she forgot. Finally, she told him there was a thing at a loft but he'd have to pay to get in. The crowd swayed and yelled. Cigarettes, pills. More students. He was hot, sweaty; he'd been surrounded by this sucking, pushing crowd before, when their faces had been masked, their voices raw. Onstage, she waggled her tongue, grinned, and pushed two more red feathers through the skin of each shoulder to flare behind her. Red rubber panties mercilessly ate her up. Her eyes were wide with makeup. Hot magenta ribboned from the single hole in her cheek down her collarbone. Her stilettos were half a size too large. As she swanned offstage she tripped and plunked to her knees like a toddler. He waited for the wail. Alone under the light, she pushed herself back up and made an ironic little curtsy.

When he met the baby in the hospital, Lucette couldn't hold it up for him to take, because the Caesarean had sliced through all her muscle. "Well, he'd feed Bucephalus for about a month," she said.

"Good lord, Lu." He hefted the baby in his arms. He rocked it.

Onstage, the white snake had sought Lucette's face with its own, anxiously tightening around her shoulders as she smilingly loosened it. Loosened it again. Popov had shifted closer through the crowd. A living noose with a yearning knob of brain at the end. The promoter came forward with arms raised to take it from her.

"Fuck's sake, she knows what she's doing," someone complained.

While feeding, the snake had lain piled on itself. He'd lifted the seven-dollar rat out of the pet-store box, thumb at the base of its skull. Its legs worked. Its heartbeat flushed warm against his fingers. He carried it, squeaking, around the apartment. He didn't take off his shoes as he watered her plants. Lucette kept all her books piled along the walls beside her bed.

The girl, Laliberté, was standing in the hall after his presentation, reading middle-school essays stapled to the wall. Medieval warfare; the Roman legion; the Holocaust.

"Did you like that?" he asked.

"Yes, Sir," she said. The cadets all said Sir, unlike the students he spoke to in daylight. She had a clear voice, an oil slick across her forehead, the height of which was accentuated by the peak of the ridiculous cap. None of them polished their boots correctly.

"Good. I need a new boss," he said, and got a smile out of her. Teeth too big for her face still.

She adjusted the belt of her tunic. "I guess everyone wants you to help them all the time."

He tilted his head. The corridor had emptied.

She said, "What kind of horse is that?"

"Cross-breed," he said.

"Where is he?"

"It's retired."

"Can you visit him?"

"Sir," he reminded her. He knew nothing bad had ever happened to her, but she would disagree.

In daylight, he saw her in the same hallway wearing the same slashed dress the girls all wore. "Sir," she said as she passed, blushing.

When Lucette had retired—her word—all that happened was she changed her phone number. She still couldn't stop checking the thing. She laughed about it and put her hair in his face as she straddled him on the sofa. "Oh my god," she said, "What an addict."

"You can't live without the attention," he said.

She'd look at him like that, without expression, sometimes, then more and more often. She kept the same passcode on her phone and her debit card, and he'd read the pleas from men who *Just need to hear your voice*. But when those messages ceased he didn't know if it was because they had stopped coming.

As he'd fed it to Bucephalus, the rat had turned on itself, tried to crawl back up its own body. The snake opened one red eye. He lowered the rat further. Jiggled it. The snap-shot strike lashed the glass and set Lucette's glassware ringing. The lizard muzzle brushed his fingers, or maybe it was just disturbed air. The snake knotted around the rat, jaw clamped to its spine, until everything stopped twitching. Then the snake began to heave, uncoiling, fitting its mouth around the rat's head, swallowing it, swallowing it for an hour.

The baby turned two. Popov's mother put money in an account, but Popov did not tell Lucette. He did not even think about telling her.

"I should leave him here with you," Lucette said. She was angry. She'd found out, finally. "What would you do then? You can't lie to him. He has to learn to talk before you can do that."

The blonde, Tereza, snorted when he explained. "I adore you," he said. "But I have to be gentle with her. She's unpredictable. It scares me."

"Perhaps you could be a little less predictable," said Tereza. She had met his mother once, too, by accident.

In the spring the cadets held their annual ceremony, and Laliberté, with new bars on her shoulders, was presented with her scholarship. She would go north and learn to fly jets. White dust from the painted yard lines further ruined the formation's boot polish. She shook the commander's hand and unfolded a piece of paper in front of the microphone. The sun broke a sweat on her. Her voice competed with the breeze and her own breath over the loudspeakers.

"I would like to thank everyone, but especially my father. When I was little he scared me. He would drive too fast. He'd take me to the woods and we'd go through barbed wire with No Trespassing signs. Once, a kid threw a rock that cut my head open and when we were driving to the hospital we saw him, biking over the bridge, and my dad stopped and he grabbed the kid and I don't know what he said to him but he held him by the collar and pushed him in my face. I remember I couldn't stop sobbing. I kept saying I was sorry. I was afraid of what would happen if anyone got angry."

The formation twitched, then cramped. A young man had dropped to his knee, dizzy, holding his cap before him as if to vomit into it. He was escorted into the shade of the bleachers that held the ranks of fathers, some in denim, some in collars, all equally grim, no single one of them looking any more exposed than the rest.

Popov caught the kid, actually. The one who had thrown the broken beer bottle that day on the mountain. The glass gashed the gelding's shoulder, and the beast screamed as they galloped up through the trees. He landed a leap over one of the stone fences that made the park so like a cemetery and the kid, hair braided to his skull, zagged in confusion. They could have run him down, talons savaging the meat of him, but instead Popov seized him by the collar, dragged him a few steps, shook him.

The kid swore and twisted, battered at Popov's arms.

On the path below, strings of people froze. Popov, sweating his blacks blacker, shook the kid again. The kid's face snarled up, his body wiry and muscled in a rag of a red shirt.

"What did you think? What did you think I'd do?" said Popov.

The kid thrashed, white-eyed. He could have pulled Popov from the saddle if he'd used his weight right, but he didn't even try.

"I'm gonna ruin your life, you get it?" said Popov.

The kid wouldn't let go of Popov's wrist. Thumbs at the tendons, he looked to the citizens.

"Why are you looking at them? My horse can tear open your asshole. Are they going to help you?"

One of them had her phone's eye raised, recording.

He radioed for a squad car, but the other mounted officer had called and one was already on its way. He locked the kid to his stirrup, walked back down the mountain. The gelding chortled to itself. Its shoulder bled two shades brighter than its coat. Blood slid down its foreleg. Popov caught the glint of its eye glancing back at their prisoner.

At the foot of the mountain, under the soaring, starry statue of Octavian, Popov jerked his foot in the stirrup so the gelding jolted and the kid stumbled, but didn't fall. The car pulled up with a single squawk. The kid clung closer to Popov's heel and the gelding's ribcage. Popov dismounted, took his pistol from its holster. "You let me treat you like this," he said as he unlocked him. He pushed him along and the kid made a show of falling to the ground. He lay there, canines bared.

Then, for a second, no one was looking, and Popov let the reins slack.

This was the summer of the riots, the summer he met Lucette. The anarchists swarmed down off the mountain, out of their northern ratholes, to pollute the sidewalks. Office girls couldn't eat lunch on public benches. Streets were fenced, but maps were unreliable, impossible to keep current, same as policies. How to disarm them? Where to put the press? Popov rode through the crowds and their voices made a vice of the air.

That first night with Lucette, she'd carried a candle and led him in procession to her low, rosy bed. Standing naked against her in her kitchen had been like standing in a perfect dream of his own future: exactly like this. Exactly.

When the crowd became black masks he was the only officer in sight. They cawed at him with torn metal voices. The gelding contorted, furious. The people roiled. One slunk close, hissed aerosol into the beast's eye. It trumpeted, reared to its haunches, slashed its claws. When it unfurled the hemisphere of its black wings, the shadow fell over them all.

Slave Craton

Erin wields the hatchet lightly, like it's lit upon her hand. The cedars here have been dead longer than they were alive. Most are fallen: whale spines crest in the grass. This piece of land dropped so suddenly into the ocean they suffocated all at once. Ever since, Erin told him, the land's been rising again.

She stops at a trunk that's crashed sideways to lie canted at hip-height. She pushes against it. Solid. Decomposing firmly into the grass. She takes one experimental swing and the hatchet glances off the wood. A chip of bark wings away.

"Good?" she grins at him. Wriggles out of her backpack.

Michael is still wearing his dirty yellow life preserver. She left hers with the kayaks. He's sweating badly. He takes it off and holds it.

"Can we eat first?" he says.

"I wouldn't," she says. "You'd just puke."

She opens the first-aid kit, passes the roll of gauze to him and wraps a wide, blue elastic band four times around the base of her ring finger. He can't avoid her eyes. She touches his wrist.

"Ready?" she says.

Her gaze has that cloudless intensity that means she is thinking about how she loves him, though she won't say it. Thank god. His gut twists: shit or eat. His hands are cold and wet. She should know better. She should be able to see into him clearly enough to stop herself.

Right hand splayed over the trunk, she swings one hard and perfect stroke with her left. Her breath releases in a high sigh.

"Can you wrap it?"

The wind in the trees is a highway roar. Blood spurts childishly.

"Michael? Can you help me wrap it?"

She missed, slightly: hit halfway between the top knuckle and the second. He hovers, but she pinces the end of the gauze and pushes it into the stump. The idea was just the top knuckle, the fingernail, essentially. Instead of a ring. Something irreversible.

"Easy," she hisses through her teeth. Sweat pools above her lip. "See? Mother fuck," she says.

"I don't think so," he says.

"It feels, oh shit, it *hurts*." Her grin comes back.

"Quick," she says.

"I can't do it for you," she says.

"Michael," she says.

The water has a slight seaward current. It slinks at the same speed as time. He doesn't look at her swabbed finger or her shining face. If he looks the entire landscape will collapse and she'll rush in like the ocean to engulf him.

He picks up his life preserver again. He takes a step back into the dead tangle. He pushes the kayak into the shallows. He leaves her like that. She will not mark him.

8/3

It was easy for him to leave the city and come to her research station on the coast—they eat at the canteen and sail out on the core-sample boat and talk to the harbour seals. He pecks at visible action items for a few hours a day to keep his project manager pleased. He sets up an automatic payment to Oxfam. Two thousand a month. At first it was one, but she asked him flat-out what his net income was and conducted some harsh math and he was forced to admit that yes, he could, technically, afford two.

"I want to promise something to you," she says in the noon sun, their lunch trash scattered around them, the escarpment dropping below into the wrought-iron tree tips, glass-green seawater. She has already explained how the horizon, after the continent snaps back, will rise up. Just a little, like an eyebrow, until it bulldozes the shore. Here, then ten hours later in Japan. A seven hundred mile wave. Even up here, looking down, it would hit them like they'd fallen ten storeys to the sidewalk.

"I don't know," she says, "Something permanent."

"I know," he says. The air is thick between them, the same strain of emotion condensed like terrarium humidity. He rests his skull against hers. His chest is a hollow earth with a burning sun inside it. His palm smoothes her inner knee, his fingers on the scars there. She has more, moony ovals, at her shoulderblades and haunches.

She says, "In the rigging, when you're floating there with the pain. It's not pain. Or I mean, it's not suffering. It holds you. It's not as fucked up as it sounds. People are addicted to worse things. Internet poker."

"It doesn't sound like an addiction," he says, thinking of Amy.

"I didn't mean addiction. It's a practice. It's better than an internet-poker practice."

"You just hang there. On the hooks," he says. The scars fan, overlap. They are neat, swabbed, repeated.

"It is not suffering," she says. "Do you know how many Lakota teenagers tried to kill themselves last winter? A hundred and three. Nine actually did it. In South Dakota. But that was in March. I read that in March." Her fingers creep and interlace with his. She noses against his neck, breathes into his skin. The word love is weather between them. He thinks it constantly. She does too, because she clings to him in the night, smiles as she opens her eyes to him. "That's suffering. This is not suffering."

"The ghost forest," she says. "Once you see it you'll never want to leave."

"Was I leaving?" he says.

She raises her eyebrow at him. She's older than he is. She knows what he's thinking before he does. She thinks more than he does. Her ideas are familiar, arterial, from his childhood. He feels so lucky to have recognized her. From a distance: a stranger who is actually kin. It was the hollows under her eyes.

"I'm here," he says.

Her face folds. She laughs into his shoulder until she turns to wipe her nose because she is crying. His sleeve is wet with tears. She laughs again, but her eyes are pink and blue. She butts her forehead under his chin. "Don't change your mind," she says. She is begging him.

12/27

No explaining the impulse to hide from the helicopter. It's not about to land in the trees here, scoop her up kicking. Scooted under a cedar with neon witch's beard in her face, Amy laughs at her hermit-crab instincts. It's the first engine she's heard. Obviously it has other priorities. Amy, ankle-deep in iced mountain bog, cradling the purse she pulled out of her car, can't quite tell how drunk she is anymore. Not at all. She must still be, though. She fell asleep briefly, lower down, against a trunk, but the ground started moving again and the idea of another wave levered her back to her feet. She pulls her pants, hangs over a branch, pisses downhill. Then she keeps climbing, hands and knees, slipping in pine-needle avalanches. Uphill, obviously. Eventually she'll see what's going on, now that daylight is happening. She wipes hair out of her face and brushes her smashed-up nose. It feels like it maybe got shoved into her brain. Her fingers are brittle twigs. Glass-cut, leaking blood on the left, she arranges them under her dirty blouse against her hot belly. "I changed my mind!" she yells after the helicopter, long gone, and laughs.

The ground changes and she crawls up the lip of a dirt road cut into the side of the mountain. It's frozen in ruts and is almost horizontal, compared to everything else. She can't see much through the trees, still. Buttery sky above. Birds chatter. She dangles her legs over the edge of the incline, opens her purse, plucks out her plastic water bottle, which is gin and flat soda. The sound of another motor.

This one an insect whine. The woman on the ATV looks as surprised as Amy.

"Where'd you come from?" she says.

"Highway." Amy points downhill.

"Jesus. You were in the wave?"

"What wave?" Amy quips. She laughs. Her hatchback, netted in trees above the road. That part of the highway was, lord, hundreds of feet above the beach. She must've just caught the crown of it, and still. She and a mudslide fell six feet back down to the ground when she opened the car door. Her feet squish in her ankle boots. She'd left the hotel in a rage. That's what it was. They'd been in the restaurant overlooking the bay. She'd ordered a third bottle and Michael had said to the waiter, *The house red is fine, no point wasting the good stuff.*

"Are you all right?" the woman says. Her braid is blonde, she has a sleepless look. She is looking at Amy with a certain intensity Amy recognizes. She means, *Are you drunk?*

"No," says Amy automatically.

"You better come back with me," the woman says. When she offers Amy her hand, it's deformed. One of the fingers is stumped short. Amy stares at it. When the woman hauls her up by the armpits, she starts to cry.

7/28

When Erin comes to the city to visit Michael for the first time there are more vegan restaurants than they could possibly go to in two days, and the one he suggests she wrinkles her nose at. "We could just cook," she says, thumbing through the menu on his front stoop, that shapeless, ratty backpack slung over her shoulder. She is wearing shorts and a spark-burnt fleece. Her hair is falling out of its braid.

"We could," he says.

"Was I right about your fridge?" she says.

He shrugs. He made an attempt to bring the place from a Level 10 disaster to a Level 7, but he doesn't say that in case she scoffs at the result.

"I just have a hard time spending that kind of money," she says. "Kale bowl."

"I'm paying, obviously," he says. He looks ahead and sees the pattern form like clouds over the street: Amy, always a week short of her pay cheque, gas for her car, phone bill overdue. On his way over to her place his phone would buzz: *bring wine?*

"That's nice, but it's the utility," she says. "You pay seventeen dollars instead of what, five? So we don't have to think or wash anything? But you could pay Unicef two hundred to turn a sick two-year-old into a reasonably healthy six-year-old."

"Yes," says Michael.

"Luxuries are just tough for me," Erin says. Her voice is apologetic but her face is not.

"You'd rather cook," he says.

"Is that obnoxious? I'm sorry."

They walk to the grocery store. Inside, he trails her until she says, an ultra-pleasant edge to her voice, "Could you go find the almonds, maybe? Whole and unsalted."

When he opens the door to his apartment, she puts the bags down on the floor. She picks up a glass from the rack. "Are these clean? Where is your cutting board?"

He putters uselessly, trying to pick a record and make it play while she chops and clatters. She rinses dishes he washed that morning, but he doesn't say anything. Her focus is silent, intimidating. "Is that a door? Can you open it?" she says, gesturing to the balcony with the knife.

"Okay," he says. Then, "Why?"

"It's a little stuffy?"

"They were cutting grass outside earlier. I had to shut it."

"That seems counterintuitive," she says.

"I'm allergic," he says.

She smiles without looking at him, but it's more of a sneer. He wants to walk up behind her, press his hard-on to her ass and wedge the blade of his hand between her legs, but she does not seem to like him right now. It's possible she'll eat dinner then leave. It's possible she'll leave.

"You don't have to stay," he says.

"What?" she stops cutting. A beet falls to the floor. She ducks under an open cabinet door to look at him.

"I just—like, if you don't want to," he says.

"I just drove for two hours."

"Do you want to be here?" he says.

"Do I? Are you actually asking me?" she says. She puts the knife down and steps from the linoleum to the parquet. She didn't take off her sandals. He hadn't managed to sweep. "Yeah, wow, okay, that was fast," she says to herself. "Clearly this is who you are."

Stepping out of the kitchen means she's stepped towards the door. He imagines her on the other side of the closed door, down the steps, on the sidewalk.

"I'm sorry," he says. He steps towards her, one hand up.

"You haven't even touched me since I got here," she says.

He kisses her. She backs into the counter. She whines. On the couch, she puts her mouth on his cock. He takes off her tank and brushes the scars that float over her shoulder blades like islands. She unrolls a condom and the light goes. Then she pours a beer, with a self-conscious glance at him, and resumes cooking under the stove light. Bare-chested, he watches from the couch. A slow-boiling sun of emotion rises in his ribcage, watching her move in his space. They eat kale and quinoa on the balcony in the hot dark, the trees brushing their feet, the neighbour's eternal Bob Marley drifting up.

"You only need twenty-five thousand to live," she says. "Or in my case, fourteen because the government houses me so much of the year. The rest can go."

Michael nods, letting his knee rest against hers.

"It's none of my business, but people are starving to death and we all have the fucking phone number for Oxfam. No one can honestly plead ignorance."

"That guy outside the grocery store," Michael says. "Every day. It's like a job. It's like community service he's doing. Every time I see him I know where I am, where I live."

"He wouldn't ask for money if he didn't need it," she says. "No one would ever ask, is the thing people don't understand. Just by merit of asking you for money that guy has proved that he needs it more than you do. Because you've never had to ask, have you? Random luck means you've never had to ask."

"I give him twenties, sometimes," says Michael. "Randomly. Now there are days when I give him change and he was expecting a twenty. Maybe he's counting on it that day, I don't know. I don't know what he needs. Just saying it diminishes it."

"You could ask him. You could buy him lunch."

"I don't want to though," he says. "That would feel condescending. I'd rather just pay."

"You can, though, is my point," she says.

"Could you stay?" he says. The sun, expanding like that, it could choke him. "This weekend? Until you really have to go. Could you stay on Monday?"

"No." She grimaces. "I have another cycle to start running at ten a.m. What about you? You work remotely sometimes?"

"Yeah, anywhere," he says. "I only go in because—" he waves a hand at the disaster inside: the silty floor, the hair and dust over the undergraduate textbooks.

"So come back with me."

"Yes," he says. The cedars out there, warm as good parents. What if he left forever? His project manager, his boss. His colleagues untangling his gnarled code. Apartment deep in dust. "For a couple of days."

"I'm scared," she says into his collarbone, later, in the dark. They are slimed, limp, paddling on the sunny surface of sleep. "This is the thing you don't turn away from."

7/20

He stays, and in the morning Erin lies in her cot, stinking of hangover. "Would you like some water?" he says. She mumbles. He fills her bottle from the huge plastic canister in the kitchenette. She rolls over and slits her eyes. "There's aspirin," she points. He fetches it.

The little mattress is too narrow to welcome him back, so he dresses in yesterday's muddy clothes—it was too presumptuous and too hopeful to pack a spare set—kisses her slick temple and silently settles the screen door into its warped frame.

The morning's mildness is already baked dry. Grass roasts under his boots. He pauses at the curve of the hill between her hut and the rest of the station, not knowing where to go. The islands hump around in the ocean's flat black. The clouds are stacked vertically all around him, like friendly gods. He needed coffee hours ago. He does not want to go out on the core-sample boat. He tries not to feel manipulated. He tries to enjoy the sunshine.

When he was a kid he dreamt that the volcano had woken up, and the red light coming in through his curtain was the heat death of the universe. He ran the tub full of cold water and sat in it until his dad came in, hairy. His dad was mean when surprised.

There's an insect buzzing like a drone, so loud it must be the size of a raven. Or maybe there are just many of them, and he's surrounded. He will not make the same mistake. This does not feel like the same mistake. He will not love another drunk. But Erin is not a drunk, she just got drunk. He is not scared.

He creeps back into her hut to grab his bag. He'll call later, apologize, say something came up with work. She's dressed, though. She splashes water on her face. Long legs. Long, dirty feet. She cocks her head at him, water drips from her chin. She looks five years older: lines have appeared where there were none. But they are kind lines, they welcome him to live in them. "Guarding the perimeter?"

"All clear," he says. The curve of a scar flashes like a grin at her knee. "What are those from?"

"Suspension," she says.

"Like, hooks?"

"It's kind of a hobby. Sanitized. Industrial rigging. Some people do yoga."

"But you don't have any tattoos."

She pads over to him, curls her fingers fondly around his wrist. "Out of the mouths of babes." She puts his fingers in her mouth, flicks her tongue against the tips.

"I'm not that young," he says.

"Virgin," she says. "Baby."

Lying down with her curled against him he says, "In sixth grade I made a vow to make as much money as I could so that I could buy up the rainforest before it was all cut down. It was a school day. The moon was out at eight a.m. I promised it to the moon."

She doesn't say anything. For a long time her fingers stroke the web of his hand. He is sleepy. She murmurs his name into his ear, a heartbroken little voice that stirs the roots of his spine.

12/27

The woman drives Amy to a house in a clearing. They judder over a cattle guard, and there's also a garage, solar panels, a greenhouse, several other small and specific buildings. Everything roofed in black aluminum. A two-strand barbed-wire fence skirts the property, and there's a much higher fence around some trees and raised vegetable beds.

"I knew you were out there," the woman says, killing the engine. She helps Amy step down from the perch she's frozen to. "Bath, maybe?" she says, "Tank's twelve hundred gallons so don't be shy."

She leaves Amy to sit, tit-deep, in warm water. Dripping, Amy digs around in her bag to find the plastic water bottle, then settles back into the tub. She sips.

When she wakes up it's dark out and the clock says 04:12. The woman's reclining in an easy chair. A man on the radio says, "Total devastation miles inland rescue crews say thousands—"

"I have to go see if I can find anyone else, or what's the point," says the woman. The chair creaks as she pushes herself out of it. She hits a light switch. "But fucked if I didn't tell those assholes."

"How bad is it?" Amy says. A headache drifts somewhere above her skull, looking for a place to settle.

"Nine point four," says the woman. She pours water into a coffee press.

"My fiancé is in Open Court Bay. You know the resort there?"

The woman gazes at her. "No chance," she says. Her stub finger taps the counter as the beans grind. Outside, the trees start to appear as pale lines against their own dark. It's raining.

Amy sits. He'd moved in, like she'd wanted. They'd talked about meetings, until they didn't. Walking out every few weeks is part of the passion. She's always believed in passion.

The woman hands her a rough, heavy mug. "The plate just bent and bent," she is saying. "I told them. The Slave Craton's the oldest rock on the planet. It doesn't move. It was never going to move. Something else had to."

7/16

As soon as he can, he rents another car and drives out to the research station, passing the spot where Erin first swiped his teeth with her tongue, just days ago but already time is expanding, slowed down with the added weight. When he pulls into the parking lot, Erin greets him with an awkward wave. She stands at a professional distance so he can't quite find a way to kiss her. She smiles like he's arrived to update software. The facilities are both more and less rustic than he'd imagined: layers of outdated technology washed up in the ebb and flow of funding. DVD spindles and Windows Vista. The core-sample boat is a royal blue rust giant that stinks of headache. Erin's eyes dart between him and everyone they meet as she tours him around. He is happy to see that the drilling tech whose opaque wisecracks she is always relaying—*Marco says I can make it as a synchronized rip-chain puller*—is round and wears a necklace of wooden beads under his ornate facial hair.

"I hope you brought bourbon," says Marco as they shake hands. "Because it's bourbon night and tomorrow is hangover fishing."

"He's joking," Erin deflects. "But we can go out on the boat tomorrow, if you want."

Michael doesn't answer.

"I mean, if you're staying?" she says.

Marco hoots and walks off.

"Am I?" says Michael. The sun's already burnt his left forearm through the closed window on the drive here. He tries to cover the scalded skin with his other hand.

"I hope so," says Erin, "I'm inviting you."

She opens the screen door to her hut and he puts his bag down on the marshy linoleum. It smells of mould and pesticide, but the dry breath of the cedars sighs through a huge back window and it's cooler in here, a little.

She tugs at the bedspread: "I can fifty percent guarantee no spiders."

He came here to kiss her. He walks up behind her, puts his hands on her waist. "Hm," she says, and backs into him so his hands run up her ribs. Her back is arched. She's wet to the touch. The air streams through the screens of latched door and dusty window, and she shushes him once, twice. Naked, she is soft. The scars run in pairs down the dorsal lines of her body. He doesn't ask. He comes too quick. He works on the right architecture. Every time she says, "Hey listen," he pushes her back down and continues. She's not that difficult. He shushes her sardonically. The crocheted blanket is a hot swamp. Her hair is a trash tide over her head and he laughs about it while she laughs. Her eyes are black-blue, he thumbs the dark circles under them.

When they open the door to her hut the sun has dumped itself into the strait under a sediment of war-red clouds. She glances around and he pulls her close to inhale her licked-clean throat. "Okay," she pushes him off. "I work here."

As promised, she carries half a bottle of bourbon. She drops his hand as they find other people—the migration biologists—at the top of the escarpment, and everyone skids down a hundred-foot dirt chute step-laddered with stripped roots.

He hasn't eaten since breakfast. He has his steel water bottle and now, muddy shorts.

They approach an ancient rite: muzzy, stinking bonfire ringed by blackened stones and vandalized logs. High tide, he'd guess, with the trees hanging over. The waves cough and push flocks of insects around. A dozen people talk through the flames. They find a spot beside Marco. The trunk they sit on is so thick it must've been two hundred years old. Now it's carved and painted. POISON ALL POLLUTERS KILL ALL POACHERS.

"How's the hike? You make it to the waterfall? You guys look pretty satisfied," Marco cackles at another guy in a baseball cap as he pierces a corner-store hot dog with a whittled spear. Erin takes a protein bar out of her backpack. He snorts at it. "You're missing out."

"Don't talk to me about that thing," she says, taking a swig of the bourbon. The sausage looks small and pissy. Michael finds it unlikely that she will want to kiss him if he eats one.

"So you're into seismology, too?" Michael says.

"Sure," says Marco. " I was doing deep-sea oil wells before, but this pays the same and is way fuckin' easier, no offense."

"Marco is post-ethical," says Erin. "He could give a shit how many kids are about to die because the government won't move any schools out of the inundation zone. No matter what my estimates say."

"Hey Erin, tell me again how smart pigs are?" says Marco, squirting mustard. He hands a hot dog to Michael without asking. Erin looks at it. Then she gives him a tiny, bitter salute with her bottle.

"Easier to believe that I'm exaggerating than that I'm right. Ten to one, right? That's the odds? How about this year? What would they do if I say it'll happen by December thirty-first?"

"Shut up, Erin," says Marco. "Michael, please help yourself to condiments."

7/10

Their first date is at a diner at a misty little stoplight halfway between what she's described as her coastal hut and what he hasn't admitted is a wreck of a downtown apartment.

"So why don't you drink?" she says. "Medication?"

He sips his coffee, frowns. "I need a reason?"

"Sorry," she says. "Was that pushy? No, of course you don't."

She has black circles under her eyes. He hadn't really noted how tall she was at first, shoulder-height on him. Her hair splinters at the ends. He'd believe it if she said she used to train birds of prey. Her hand describing a swift, euphoric *up!*

"Do you want to guess my thing, then?" she says.

"What, that you're vegan? That's not it." He shakes his head. "I have no idea."

"It's obvious," she says. "If you were paying attention at all."

"I guess I wasn't."

Her eyes widen. She reaches across the table to thumb the web of his hand. "Don't apologize. I'm just a harpy."

He smiles. "You don't scare me."

She laughs so loudly that the waitress rolls her eyes. She grimaces, pushes her water glass with a finger. "I'm so much older than you."

"And I'm such an innocent," he says, "Nubile ingénue. Corruptible." He has the advantage of being skinny and tall, and he gets his hair cut at a good place, but there are some symptoms of himself that are hard to hide, like how his hands tremble, how his eyes are puffy under thick lenses, and how he has lost people over the years. He read her dissertation online—or at least skimmed the abstract, scrolled through the methodology. "So you transferred from Alaska?"

"Two years ago."

"Wouldn't you rather be elsewhere, considering what you know is going to happen?"

"It's my job," she says. "I'll survive."

"Will I?" he says.

"Depends." Her smile is tiny. It travels through him, over the trees, up the knobbed spine of the coastal range. "Stick with me, kid," she drawls.

He laughs a little, to dispel the chill.

She cocks her head. "So you were in love."

"Like, recently?" he says. The water glitters in its glass.

"A year ago, two. It was intense," she says. She leans forward. "You abased yourself. She blacked out most nights. You lost your friends. You were together for what, a year and a half, before you realized you'd kill yourself if you stayed? But she kept begging you back, and it was another two years before you stopped letting her convince you. You'll never know if anything she ever said was true."

Something rattles in his sternum. He is stopped. Fingers cold against the coffee cup.

"I'm right," she says. "I know when I'm right."

He considers the possibility that this woman has been sent as some kind of vengeance. By Amy. By the universe. But his therapist says that kind of paranoia has to be breathed into. He presses his fingers to the bones of his chest. A sun beats through the thin skin there. It burns towards its end.

Moriah

In 1828 certain men of this village climbed to the peak of Mount Isaac to eat the yolk of the great roc's egg. Yet the savage bird came upon them and, as they fled in their vessel across the lake, dropped boulders and trees from on high until all their rapacious souls were drowned.

"Vengeance"
bronze cast, 1848, H. Simon Dodge
Town square, Moriah, N.Y.

On Saturday she drove the book bus down to the mineside cottages and served every man who came. They were waiting for her on their porches, rockbound between rusted cliff and shoreline algae, holding last week's books. By the time she parked, unbuckled herself, and folded her laminate desk down, they had formed a silent line. She propped open the door and Victor, with his flabby hips and goose-honk woman's voice, stumped up the steps first. He shuffled down the corridor of spines, hunched under the low roof, examining titles. Next came Tyler, polite and handsome. He should've been in college. "Did you get the next *Henry*?" he asked her.

Moriah retrieved *IV, Part II* from the milk crate at her feet.

Below, Matthew was crowding up the steps to browse the nearest titles on the bottom shelf. His body filled the door, dimming the light and lacing her veins tighter.

"Matthew," she said.

He had a sucker's scowl, and his dark eyes held white points as if they contained a smaller animal's flashlit glare within them. But he obeyed. He stepped back down to the dirt and the line flexed behind him.

Every week Moriah rotated the collection from the library's stock. The men liked their success memoirs, sexy horrors, world records, and sociological histories. Tyler was working through Shakespeare, and took an occasional showy jab at poetry. Victor preferred self-help and science fiction. None of them worked; no one would hire them. Three books each, every week, and every week each asked for more. There was no imagining their boredom.

As each man passed by her desk with his new selections, Moriah tore up last week's record. No database: stamps and slips only. Her system's amnesia was a point of professional pride. A few liked to ask her advice. Keller, for instance, who'd taught business courses and spoke at a volume set for three hundred students, read only what she picked for him.

Rain rattled the bus roof. Each man dropped back to the dirt like a mother, shoulders curled over his books, and bolted for his den.

Adrian stepped up last, with his skinny, burnt-out body and bald ostrich skull. He liked non-fiction mostly, popular history on sea voyages and polar expeditions, gold rushes, disease. He read the mass-market series with bent and foggy covers, or else dug up some close-kerned text from the fifties with a waxy canvas spine, something a decade overdue for weeding and the municipal bonfire. At the back of the bus, where the emergency exit was the only window not walled-over in paperbacks, she planted treasures for him. This week, a battered edition of *One Thousand and One Nights*, illustrated, and an account by an Arab secretary of his dealings with Viking traders in the tenth century. Adrian plucked them unerringly. Also, his own personal choice: *White Fang*.

"Again?" she said.

He shrugged. He almost smiled.

She noted each of the titles. She slid last week's slip across the desk to him, untorn, because the first time she'd come, or actually the second, he'd said, "Wait," when he realized what she was about to do. "Could I have it?" he'd said.

He wrote his name with a left-hander's limp: wrist curled to protect the broken letters as they formed. She slid the books back to him. She wore dark blouses to camouflage the wet circles under her arms. Inside her sleeve, sweat ran down her tricep. If they could smell her nerves they did not let on.

"Enjoy," she said to Adrian. She said it to all of them.

She closed the door behind him and reversed the bus through the rutted dirt, which was softening dangerously in the rain. But instead of turning onto the main road back to town, she steered up the grassed and lumpy left fork. The trailhead was just a gravel lot with a sign that read MOUNT ISAAC. Deserted. There were trees to mask the bus' obvious yellow from passing vehicles, her neighbours, the other men who lived in the cottages. She killed the engine and opened the door to the wet air and gleaming branches.

At the back exit, she settled spine-to-spine with the books on a painted footstool left over from when the bus had served communities flooded with children. The window was a siltscreen, streaming mud. Wind crabbed the poplars. She stroked her hair from crown to throat, and was soothed.

On foot, Adrian plucked his hood up and took the long path to meet her. He was never sure. The first time he'd found her, he'd been carrying his new books to read in the trees and discovered her in her habit of sitting alone. He'd stood in the clearing. She'd opened the door.

Her hair was fine and listless. She closed her eyes and pinced the hem of her skirt as he crouched and spread her bare knees. Her skin, in the damp, was goosepimpled, and he palmed her calves to warm them.

"You should wear something warmer," he said.

Her mouth twisted. "It's August."

One hand on her thigh, he pulled aside white lace to rub the fingers of the other inside her. She always started so slick for him, but it still took her such a long time, every time, before she forgot him enough to sob and buck, then lean down to cup his ears and kiss his crown.

As he licked her, his knees grated against pebbles on the plastic mat. His hooked back ached. His tongue numbed. He didn't shift around. He kept licking. He tasted blood. He ignored it. He wouldn't embarrass her. In fact, he liked it, how she would stop him as soon as she realized, apologetic. But then it wasn't just a taste but a gush, wetter than even her usual mess, and ferric, and he drew back to look at the gore smearing her thighs. She opened her eyes. "Oh, God!"

He lifted a hand to his face and red splashed the back of it.

"Your nose!" she crowed, one wrist to her mouth, one hand reaching for him. She laughed.

"Shit," he said. The white lace was an abattoir rag. Blood purpled the blue of his shirt. "I thought it was you."

"No, I don't, really," she twisted a wrist, still laughing, "bleed, ever."

She closed her knees and he followed her out. His hands shone, savage. She dug a bottle of water out of her purse, and tipped it over his face. He held his hands out to the rain, which was too sparse to help. She pressed dusty tissues to the blood still streaming from his nose, and he pinched the bundle there himself. She hovered on the bus steps, grinning, her fingers pink, her face pink.

"I don't know what," he said.

She giggled, again. She used a finger to hook the ruined lace down her legs, and stepped out of it. His blood rubbed her ankles.

"I'm so sorry."

"Don't be."

"Can you clean them?"

He reached, but she didn't pass them to him. She held them under the diminishing rain herself. "Of course."

"Don't throw them out."

"I wouldn't," she said. "Why? Do you want them?"

He paused.

"I'm joking," she said.

She kissed his cheek, and tried for his mouth despite the tissues, and laughed again when he shied. She climbed back into her driver's seat. He gathered his collar but didn't turn up his hood as he watched the bus bumble back up to the road. His blood in her, smearing the inside of her skirt, dotting her shoes. The panties balled up on the mat. The stain setting. His blood streaming from the lump of lace under cold water in her kitchen sink. His blood, antiqued to brown, locked in the fibre of the thread in the dark drawer of some bureau in a room in the house in which she lived. He never got hard for her, but she'd never been in a position to notice, which meant he had never disappointed her.

Adrian had heard about the village in its second year, was the sixth man to arrive. He spent his days grading the gravel foundations of the cottages, investigating the generator when it guttered, taping plastic over the windows. He carried a knife in his belt. He'd fenced and filled some raised vegetable beds where the spur line used to run the ore carts from the blast furnace. That was last spring; this year the boxes wheedled with radishes, the soil sunk, the boards greyed.

When he opened the door to his cottage, the others stayed quiet in their bedrooms. He lived with Tyler, who had dated a sixteen-year-old when he was twenty-one and put videos of her blowing him on the internet when she dumped him. And Matthew: rape and battery of a minor, three minors, girls he picked up in his truck and wouldn't let out again. Adrian took off his boots in his bedroom. His new books, the ones he'd had to hunt like eggs, waited on his mattress. She could easily put them on the shelf at the front, or keep them reserved in the milk crate for him like she did the others, but instead she swapped smashed spines and left it to him to note what was new. He'd never asked her to visit him here. Not with Tyler and Matthew. When he opened the door to his little house, what he missed most was calling "Hello?" and having someone rush to behold his beloved face.

Her father's house, which stood at the top of four dozen crumbling stone steps and had a plaque from the historical society mounted beside the mailbox, had passed to her, like everything else, when he died. It looked out over the lake: sailboats, the distant arc of the new bridge, the lighthouse, the monument, the blunt green mountains. And north, across the bay, the sex offenders squatting in their shacks under the dead iron mine. Coppery seams of dirt slid down to the shore from the mine's abandoned airshafts. When she was a teenager, boys would climb up there with driftwood and the caves would glow orange. Her father might not have looked up from his book for an hour, but as soon as he did he'd ring the foreman out of bed. For twenty years the miners' cottages decomposed, then, three summers ago, the men showed up. Just a few, but more arrived every year. Over two dozen now. The law was clear about where they could live. No parks, schools, public swimming pools, bus stops within a thousand yards. Moriah had none of these things. Moriah was childless.

Some days, she'd look out over the lake and see the roc: an eagle the size of a 747, hump-backed like a dromedary, white-feathered, one-eyed, circling for serpents that went extinct a century ago.

Moriah kept the habit, even after her father's death, of walking to town on Sunday and sitting at one of the three restaurants there. She was spooning her soup when Tyler passed by the plate glass. He carried his satchel over one shoulder, heavy with his new *Henry*, his dark hair wet at the temples from the afternoon sun and the long trek up from the lake. The walk itself wasn't illegal. Perhaps it took him an hour. But the men's requirements were specifically ordered, delivered, parcelled out. Usually when they walked, Adrian had told her, they walked north along the shoreline, or up the trail towards Mount Isaac, not into the town's petty core.

Tyler crossed the square to Delia's, where he could order a coffee or an ice cream, if he had the money. He leaned against the burgundy clapboard, squinting. The bronze statue of the roc claimed the centre of the square, warm and green: she was depicted as a streaming, molten creature, the ship below her splintering under a buckshot of boulders the size of elephants. One of her wingtips brushed the lake's surface as she wheeled away, beak split wide with hate. Her missing eye was gouged empty. Moriah had heard her scream once, a plummeting pitch, black as the mine's whistle. The windows of her father's library had wavered in the blare. That was another unhappy gift from her father: the key to the cold blast furnace and its silent steam-whistle.

Tyler stared at the statue like a tourist. He had an open throat and flushed cheekbones, long legs, and loafers. Just looking at him, no one would guess where he'd come from. But the government database was freely accessible, searchable by county and street, by name, and its controlled vocabulary had an Old Testament omniscience that treated privacy like a perversion. When Moriah had volunteered to drive the bus on Saturdays, her preference was to know nothing. Sometimes, though, they insisted on telling her. Adrian said Tyler talked too much, Matthew not enough.

One of the Tanner girls came out of Delia's, aproned and bunned, and stepped to the curb between bougainvilleas. She lit a cigarette and Tyler watched her inhale. He came forward and she turned as he spoke. She passed him a smoke, then lit it for him. He said something else. She replied. Tyler kept speaking, and she laughed. The girl knew what he was, but she grinned boldly. Moriah knew how pleasing it was to imagine it would be different, this time, with you.

Moriah lay her napkin on the clean tablecloth. The cook's wife refilled her tea, but didn't press the bill. Some other customers came in. Parents and their two children, passers-through.

Tyler peered into his bag and handed the girl a pen. He produced a book, flipped through it until he'd selected a page to offer her. She scribbled, returned the book, scuttled back into Delia's. Tyler sat down on a bench. He lit the second cigarette he'd begged off her. He ripped the page from the book and studied it. He folded it twice. The torn book, Moriah saw, was the Keats she'd handed him yesterday.

Her father had lived his last year entirely in his study, sleeping on a cot. When she came down in the morning, she found windows open, his books turning their own pages. She'd promised the house to the historical society. Yet here she was, still living in it. She'd kissed his hot and waxy forehead, his shoulder bared at the open neckline like a woman's. He died in his nightgown, on the floor. Her father, who told her the town had been named after her, a hundred years in advance of her birth.

Wednesday evening the grocery van arrived. Adrian was at the front of the line as Keller, fatly sweating in the breeze, sorted the cardboard boxes and white plastic bags on the rocks. He scraped at his paper with a ballpoint. The driver sat smoking out his window, engine idling, gazing across the water to town, where the painted houses striated the slope in turquoise and ochre. A few pleasure boats shrugged around at the jetty.

Keller, who'd been king of his classroom once, governed the lists and handed the driver his hundred and fifty dollar fee. The driver, Luke, re-counted the singles and fives in his lap, slowly. He'd delivered their groceries from the beginning, even when storms iced over their dirt drive and they had to clamber up the slope like goslings, handing cash and produce up and down the line. Normally, he got out of the van, made a few jokes, talked football with those who cared. They'd started to care.

"This is sick," Luke said to the money in his hand.

Keller laughed. "What, you want another raise?"

"No," said Luke. He flicked his cigarette onto the ground, where it continued to burn. Men swivelled to eye it. "I don't want shit from you."

Keller cocked his head, his smile frozen.

Adrian shifted. In line behind him, men plucked at bags, examined contents.

"I don't get it," said Keller, careful and amiable. "You want to—"

"You sickos feed your own asses," Luke said. His eyes flicked along them: a ragged string of men in faded clothes, varying hygiene; men who chose to line themselves up.

"What's that fucking mean?" said Matthew. He stepped sideways.

"You heard me, pervert," said Luke.

Matthew stalked up to the van window, but let Keller shift his bulk between them.

"Matthew," said Keller.

"What's happening?" squawked Victor from the back of the line.

"Why don't you just tell us what happened, Luke?" Keller couldn't help it, his natural mode was condescension.

"We'll figure it out," said Adrian.

"Yeah, what happened, Luke?" mocked Matthew.

Luke's lip twisted. "Like you don't know."

"No," said Keller. "Obviously we don't."

"Pussy doesn't know shit," said Matthew.

"The sheriff just picked up that kid," said Luke.

"What kid?" said Matthew.

"Letting you people stay here like this," said Luke. "We all knew what would happen."

"What did he do?" said Adrian.

"They found her up the twenty," said Luke. "Before anyone even knew she'd gone. We should've kicked you out when you first showed up. We should've made her get rid of you." His eyes flicked to the sky over the lake.

"Did he hurt her?"

"Who's hurt?"

"Moriah?" said Adrian.

"Tyler?" said Keller. "Are you talking about Tyler?"

"The old boys are done with you. They're calling her down," said Luke.

"Who are we talking about? Who is she?" Adrian pushed in, impatient.

"She's a sixteen-year-old girl, you sick fucks," said Luke.

"Is she hurt?" Keller repeated.

Luke glared. "He's gonna end up worse."

"You think?" said Matthew, pushing. "How do you think you'll end up?"

"Matthew, Jesus," said Keller, pushing him back.

"What the fuck are you gonna do?" said Luke to Matthew.

Matthew bounced. "Get outta your little car," he cooed.

"I warned you," said Luke. "I warned you. That's all you get."

He grated the van into gear. The tires kicked dust and pebbles into the produce.

Keller adjusted his glasses. Then he took them off and polished the lenses with the tail of his denim shirt, which was wet in patches. The lake smelled warmly green.

Driftwood clattered at the waterline. High above the lake, the roc drifted on mile-long wings.

For years, Adrian had spent his summers out west in a fire tower. Shifts in the cupola lasted as long as daylight, time cut to facets by radio check-ins every twenty minutes. The furred horizon was tortoise-shelled with passing clouds. The stray dog that came out of the woods went right back into them. The truck full of locals that drove up one July tried to shout him down from the tower. They had gasoline and rifles. They knew his name. He had the radio. He pulled up his ladder. They toppled his water barrel, cut his trash down from the tree, tore up his cabin, pissed his bed. He perched, silent. They could see him up there, but the red plastic jugs stayed in the truck bed. The rifles were handled, but not fired. Hours after they left, the ranger came by. She didn't get out of her truck.

He could've never got the job again, anyway. That was years ago, before the conviction.

"We can't stay here," he said. Men lingered on the rocks, nowhere to go but their mattresses. Matthew tore through his grocery bag, swearing at nothing. Victor sat on a flat rock and opened a package of strawberry wafer cookies.

The roc floated higher. Her copperplate eye watched their mouths move from two miles off. If she landed on the interstate bridge the trusses would bow. If she stooped to pass her airliner body overhead, the shacks wouldn't hold through the hurricane. Even farther above, atop the peak, her naked egg gleamed.

The sheriff stood in uniform at Moriah's door with his hat off and sunglasses on. He hadn't caught his breath from the steps. The Tanner girl was at home now, and safe. Tyler was in lock-up. They'd only made it a few miles.

"Which *act*, specifically, is assault, Robert?" said Moriah. The sun sparked the lake behind him.

"We don't need your permission," he said, though all of it was hers: the whistle, the mine, the land. "You know we'll just go in there and fire it up."

The key to the blast furnace lay in a desk drawer. She stared at him for so long he grew impatient, and reached for the door to widen it. The man's hand approaching riled something fanged in her. She shut the door hard.

When her father had been alive, he'd chaired the meetings she'd never been invited to attend. Now they'd light the furnace to sound the whistle, now they'd call her down, and Moriah had no say at all.

When she arrived at the cottages, Victor sat reading on his stoop. The windows shivered in the lake wind. The shoreline was empty.

"Victor?" she said.

"They stole most of the books," he said. "I told them. These are the ones they left."

She blinked: he had a stack of two dozen beside him.

"Maybe they'll have to burn them," he added.

"Where did they go?" she said.

He gestured upwards: the mountain.

"Everyone?" she said.

"They left hours ago. But they'll come back," he said. "Tyler won't, right?"

The steps to Adrian's front door bowed under her. There was no deadbolt, like whatever was inside was guaranteed to be worthless. She paused in the hall: three white bedrooms with white mattresses and yellow pillowcases. In the kitchen, Matthew froze, one hand deep in his stuffed knapsack. All the cupboard doors were splayed.

"Matthew," she said.

"Cunt," said Matthew. "Fuck yourself, cunt." He'd consumed her entire yellowed collection of Edgar Rice Burroughs. *Tarzan the Untamed. Tarzan and the Ant Men. Tarzan at the Earth's Core.* The kitchen was barely a closet. She took a step back. Another one. She'd never looked at the database, where it was described: aggravated sexual battery, assault, the acts contained therein. Just reading it, a violence.

She raised her hands. "It's fine," she said. She glanced into one of the bedrooms. His, or Adrian's, or Tyler's, all indistinguishable from one another. The air shifted, turned over to reveal the smell of something bacterial in the sheets. She wanted him to stop looking at her with his pinpricked eyes. She didn't turn her back on him as she retreated.

"Are you going to take these?" Victor waited outside. He held his returns: *Radical Acceptance. How to Fall Out of Love. Jurassic Park.*

"Keep them," she said.

Matthew exited the shack without looking at them. He set off up the dirt to the main road. If he walked along it, he'd be plucked up so easily. Moriah didn't call to warn him. Behind him, the door drifted open again.

"You should leave," she said to Victor. "It's not safe."

"I can't hurt anyone," said Victor, who'd gang-raped a girl when he was fourteen. He was right, though. The sheriff had told her how, forty years ago, Victor's mother and the town doctor had made sure of it.

The trail up Mount Isaac began in the clearing. Adrian looked away from the empty lot where he had found the bus, and her in it, so many times. "It doesn't go anywhere," he said to Keller. "Just up."

"Well, that's not entirely true," said Keller. "The egg is up there."

The men carried their groceries and belongings in the same plastic bags. They were rich in plastic bags, thanks to Luke. Keller wore his white sneakers and a sagging backpack. Someone had emptied Tyler's abandoned satchel and filled it with tins. Adrian had his duffel and his knife. They didn't speak as they walked. The path, which started as a wide, pine-needled boulevard, narrowed to a goat trail that skirted ledges and hopped up rock. In places, steps had been built. Crossing a stream, there was a bridge made from a fallen trunk. The late light candled the undergrowth.

Adrian took off his jacket and carried it. The sun set and he put it back on. The trees greyed. The clearing he chose had a trickle of water seeping from a rock face, which he told them not to drink until they'd boiled it. He'd brought a pot. No one else had. They'd all have to eat and drink out of their torn-lipped cans. "Get some branches," he told them. "Make a circle with those rocks." He showed them how to tie together a lean-to shallow enough that the heat would stay close. They were docile, most of them, and excited. They waited to be directed. Keller, wearing his blanket like a lord's furs, repeated Adrian's instructions in a voice that got them buzzing around the clearing.

The air dimmed into something uneasy. The fire, tentative and then suddenly fat and overfed, spat orange into the sky.

"It's too big," said Adrian.

"It'll go down," said Keller. "It's all right."

The men were ravenous. They hung skewered and foiled meat in the flames, dropped tins of beans in the embers. They pulled candy, cakes, bread, pickles, fruit, and fish in oil from their bags. They tramped through the underbrush, gathered more wood, and argued over who got to wail the hatchet down into it. They yelled and laughed like drunk miners in the black beyond the fire's halo. Keller, juicebox in hand, sang in a full baritone.

"They'll come after us," Adrian said.

They ignored him. Their shadows limped around. They yowled.

The sun was setting when the roc flew over Moriah's head. Her passage bent the trees. Pinecones and twigs rained down. Moriah looked up to glimpse her underbelly, one wing pink-tipped, the primaries splayed and curling up, the other wing lost beyond the treetops. A bull elk twisted in the wrought-iron cage of her talons. Its mouth gaped with inaudible bellows. The whistle hadn't sounded yet. It took time to kindle the furnace, work up the critical steam. Moriah had no doubt she would hear it. It would ring the rocks.

She hurried on, but the path was steep. She did not like to be travelling away from home during twilight, and she paused at a ledge as the sun dropped behind the peak. The sky grew serious while she crouched and stroked her hair from crown to throat. The dead light made the sky a hollow dome, not unlike the cave of her body, where she cozied herself, the little child, the one who always required such a long, slow process of soothing.

She continued along the path by feel, her ankles bent by roots and rocks. It was full black by the time she heard them, smelled their smoke. She came into the clearing, one arm raised to protect her face from swiping branches.

Adrian, on the far side of the blaze, stood up, peered into the darkness at what she might be.

The whistle's shrill stopped the air. The black turned to glass. It cracked against every peak and came back at them—triplicated, hexed.

"Get away from the fire!" she yelled. "You idiots!"

The men swarmed confusedly, some towards her; others looked past her into the trees.

Adrian smiled as he recognized her.

They had never shared a meal. Every time it rained or snowed, she had imagined going to his cottage and tapping on his window, but that led to imagining how he passed his evenings, every evening, and it was too painful.

"They've called her," she said, but they didn't know what she meant.

The fire crouched to a blue glaze under the logs, then leapt up as its heart collapsed. The mountain shifted left, or down. Men were gone. Instead: a mangle of scarred yellow claws. Moriah pulled herself up out of the grass. The roc tossed and gulped a bloody body down. She struck another. Her wings crooked above, a second sky. Men rushed like mice through the clearing. She stalked forward on tree-tall legs, she pinned them, she ripped them with her beak. She flapped once to balance herself and the air cracked.

Moriah reached Adrian where he crouched, gripping the hatchet. She tugged at him. The roc turned. A membrane slid across her bronze eye. She was so old. Older than the mine, older than this fissure of a lake. She'd laid her egg when her nest rested in a swamp. The mountains had formed under her. She'd lost one eye to the muskets of the men who raided her nest, but she'd destroyed them. Her beak opened; her arrow tongue curled. Moriah had never asked, and Adrian had never told her what his crime had been. The roc turned away.

Moriah knocked the hatchet from Adrian's hands and shoved him back, towards the trees. She pushed him faster. She looked over her shoulder. The hole of the roc's empty socket glared as she snaked her neck and speared Keller— who had never paid for his students' drinks but had led the drunks home and helped them with their shoes and into bed and accepted what he took as invitations—and tore him open like a wren. She ate him in two pieces. Moriah, at Adrian's heels, fell with him into the stabbing clutter of the low trees. She seized his hand. They broke branches, pushed blind. They didn't look back.

What was left living of the men was crawling crippled around the meadow. She was delicate about gathering them in her claws. When she launched herself, the down-draft snapped trunks. The bonfire's remains roared up and jumped into the grass. She beat and hauled, lifting above the treeline into the open air. She circled the peak. Below, Moriah glowed golden, lights reflected in the lake. The roc passed close to the teetering scree where she tended her egg. She let the men fall there, into the sharp rocks. Three or four of them. They could gnaw ice and old bones until it hatched. Her diamond egg, white enough to fall through, bright enough to snowblind, filled with an evil and naked creature that breathed warmly through its shell, utterly beloved.

The Tin Luck

Merope sits in the apothecary bar in the old town. The blonde man with little eyes handsprings back onto the stool beside her and leans in to murmur, in Russian, "But will you come with me?" His wet lip brushes her ear. His taxi driver, who has been paid a retainer for three days' accompaniment, scowls. Soon, the blonde man will try to buy her more whisky. She will tell him to drink it. He is not Nyman. When he tries to retain her for three days, she will laugh.

Across the bar, one of her girls has been absorbed by a tourist. Too handsome, too poor. "Too nice," Merope mutters at Irina's smile. She's right, because by dawn Merope has snapped a thumb of bills into her clutch while Irina grips a hangover.

They go to Kafé Innocents for an espresso and there is a long pause when the coffee girl asks them for three lats. "You choose," Merope tells Irina. She pulls her clutch from her purse again. "You don't wait to be plucked."

The sun is melting the snow off buildings in clumps that could fill a coffin. Only depressives and children walk the sidewalk this time of year. At least two will die by June. Merope doesn't need to look at the busted-up cobblestone of the street; the fissures are healed with packed ice. She walks en pointe. Cars take to the tram tracks.

Irina is wearing a Cossack's fur boots. The girl shuffles soggily, looking at her phone. "What are these?" says Merope, pointing to the ugly pets. "Did your friend from last night like them?"

"Did he care?" Irina wraps her hair around her throat and grimaces.

Merope slows her pace, locks her elbow into the girl's armpit to glide her. The eyes of passers-by stab her, and she stabs back, and then all the gazes fall away as if the streets were empty after all.

Agnes, Natalie, Maia, Louise, and Eva are awake, choreographed around the kettle and long table. They have agreed the rooms are best kept hot, so the apartment smells of tropical flowers, composting fruit, animal bodies. They hang their wet things from the radiators. A steam has built. The windows hold an ice glaze. It's an expense; the rooms are tall and the floors above, up to the servants' quarters on the seventh, trap heat incrementally. Merope stacks carpets and hangs tapestry curtains from October on. She'd force orchids and lemon trees in here if she could. In December they had a girl who complained of headaches and cracked the windows for fingers of cold air. Now they have Irina.

"Did you bring coffee?" says Eva as they come in. "Chocolate?"

Irina unwraps a bar and carries it to Eva, who is curled in her blanket like a spider in a rose's guts.

Agnes and Natalie have torn apart the newspaper over the long table. "They care more about the weather in 1918 than they do about what happened yesterday," Agnes snips.

"I'm going to the market," Maia says, though she is only half-dressed.

"I'll walk that way, I have a breakfast," says Louise.

In the window's unapologetic cloudlight, Merope opens her compact and brushes a lash from the creamy field of an undereye. She touches the inkline of her brow. Sometimes the snow smudges her.

Irina tracks a bog across the dining room floor, feet soaked by those useless pony boots. She closes the door to her room, which is the pantry, behind her. She's rigid: speaks on the computer to a man in Köln at ten, studies genetics until six. The man sends euros, but never comes himself. The problem, plainly, is that Irina would like to fall in love.

Merope's chair has clawed feet. It faces the window that overlooks the walk between wrought-iron fences and crook-armed acacia where all visitors and residents must file, under her, to enter or exit as they will. Her stationery is stacked on the sill. Her old brass compact rests atop, etched with leaping fawn and stag, antlers canted at a clockwork angle to the mullions. It's her security, so she can confess to her diary without troubling anyone. Maia's peasant vowels. Natalie fouling the washroom so Agnes brays. Eva, crying so fucking much. Nyman's love letters lie beneath. One of them says: *I think of you often, read: always. I am coming for you.*

On top of it all sits the twisted lump of her blackened tin luck.

Next door, the hotel was once Emilija's mansion. The snow forms grave mounds on the white marble terrace overlooking the park. A hundred years ago, Merope was a virgin in the ballroom on New Year's Eve. A waiter murmured in her ear as he refilled her champagne. She looked for her parents but no one was looking back. She trailed him up to his splintering garret. His windows were portholes, and all the house's heat had swirled up to linger there. She sweated her silk. He melted a tin toy in a ladle, poured the molten future hissing into water, and held the lump up to cast her fortune by candlelight against his wall. She peered at the shadow. Crept closer. The image steadied.

The waiter had said, as the lip of the bottle paused, dry, over her glass, "Come with me."

Tonight, Emilija's been dead for decades. Merope leaves her coat with the concierge. What was the ballroom is now a restaurant where the specialty is a gold-trimmed chocolate cake that appeals, of course, to the Russians. She has a date with Nyman.

She sits at the bar, crosses her legs and lets her wristlet dangle. The walls used to be papered with silk. The light from the Venetian chandelier would fall in warm plinks. A tiger's head passed judgment over the mantel. But now the chandelier is plastic pearls and there's a department-store Mondrian above the liqueurs. Her neighbours have all gone.

Merope takes two glasses quick and one slow. Eventually, she must allow a man near who is not Nyman.

He is short, and grinning, and wears his uniform with the evil cap. He works inside the Corner House.

"Come with me," he repeats, and gestures at the bartender.

Nyman won't show. If she climbed back up to the waiter's garret she could look through the windows across the courtyard to Nyman's windows, at the top of her own building, where the state once installed its great artists. Nyman sublets from one of them, a painter who works in an uglier neighbourhood and pockets the rent from passing internationals. The studio is efficient, with its loft bed and bookshelves like eaves-built nests, not so grand as Merope's rooms below, but hot through the winter and with a chemical smell, clean as a new government; the smell of the steam off the bath that will dissolve you.

There are so few men left in the city. Commerce drains them off like war. The women, though, are beautiful and everywhere. It's difficult for Merope to meet their eyes as they sell her gin or soap. There are better options, she wants to tell them. Instead, she lets them come to her only as they need to. Like poor Eva, clutching her paper slip with its number in the post office, sobbing. Or Natalie, mute idiot with just her English. Merope makes room for their humid bodies, an undersea pack of beaks and long arms. They bubble nets of intention that blind and confuse. They spiral upwards. They devour whole nights at a time and spit out the unpalatable survivors. They rise, never surface.

At home, Merope keeps carrots until they're limp as old men. She wraps the cheeses in layers of foil and wax and carves away the mould before nibbling. The girls will have none of it. They wail about the cupboard's rotting things as they devour corner-store chocolate with no notion of preservation, greet each other's gifts of it with new peaks of delight. But the waiter's tin luck showed her starved in the dark, and for a while she kept a terrible habit of carrying food, along with change purse and gloves, in anticipation of the day they seize her. That day, the start. She'll chew cloth, lick cement. She'll beg the locked door not to open.

Evenings in four-inch blades, Merope buys garlic at the night market. The old women quarter pomegranates to display their jewelled insides like a sturgeon's burning roe. At night, one must purchase by the box. Merope brings home her triumphs and unpacks them atop the table's long gleam. She knocks aside hairbrushes and white tapers. She lays potatoes or turnips out in sequence, like a rank and file of short-haired men: tallest at either edge, smallest in the middle. The formation tricks the eye. You see them all as equal.

From her window she used to see Nyman walk between the acacias in the dusk before five, and return at nine, or midnight, or five. The first time she went to visit him, up in his servant's room, he shied his work from her. He turned their faces to the wall.

Merope comes home from the night market with her box of hairy roots, and Agnes is crying at the door downstairs. She is angry, her mittens snotted and teary, and she glares at Merope like they've insulted each other.

"What," Merope says. She settles her box on one hip to key the door. "Why are you home?"

Agnes shakes her head. "I came back."

They walk up the steps. Merope is slow. The leather of her shoes is stiff with age. Agnes takes the box from her.

"To cry?"

"He took my purse."

"What, everything?"

"My keys. My cash, phone. My whole——"

"Before or after?"

Agnes' answer chokes her. Her mouth hangs and she closes her eyes.

In the flush of the apartment's heat, Merope presses the girl's slimy cheek to her own. "A man's presence is his power to do things to you, or for you," she says.

"This was not——" Agnes squawks. "This was not some man I met, this was——"

"A woman's presence is how she allows herself to be treated," says Merope.

Agnes pulls away. She snaps the curtain to her room, which is half the library. The other half is Maia's. Irina lives in luxe pantry solitude.

Later, Merope will twitch the curtain and offer the Soviet teapot with the gold-and-violet flowers. "Your passport?"

Agnes will rise from her book and wave a hand to where she hoards her currency, her jewellery, her documents. "I'm not stupid." Agnes has been saving to go home since they took away her teaching job the first week she arrived here. The crisis, of course, not anyone's fault. The girl's made her plane fare a few times over by now. But she lingers. Fearing the future is the only way to distinguish it from the past.

Nyman's portraits: emulsion in ice and silver halide. The thaw destroys them as they generate themselves. Poor beauties cracked and aged at the jaw, like the freeze knew where the subject's vanity had weakened her. If he had taken her portrait, Merope would see her eyes withered, her overbite skewed, her shoulders curved to collapse over her empty ribs.

"I don't know any of them," he told her. "They're just women off the street."

"You met me in the street," she said.

He laughed. He must have thought he had some kind of power, with those photographs of cracked and sagging faces.

"When I saw you, I thought you must be a school-teacher," he told her. "So straight-backed."

She lifted her eyebrows at him. When she brought him gifts of gin or whisky she'd share a glass or two, then return to find he'd drunk the bottle. The only time he called on her, her girls drifted uncertainly around him, then dispersed. They did not speak. They did not speak of him after, either.

One day, he packed his portraits in cheap pine and shipped them west.

He left.

The girls have kittenishly pushed their rents higher. They each pay tiny amounts, but as Merope has ceased to splay out her tentacles for the last dregs of men in the city, perhaps Natalie or Louise have begun to consider the amounts she must pay to live here, in the rotting street beside the boarded library and neon bathhouse. They have such little understanding of the world. Even the ones who, like her, were born in this city, who were raised to attend to the international news and the cut of their hair. Merope's parents now live in a cold part of the forest and keep their curtains closed, their television box with a blanket over it lest the deer peer in. Merope has always paid her piece to the governments. Merope had a husband once.

Against the splintering wood of the waiter's garret, the tin luck showed her the Corner House. Not the black-green arches and cavernous balconies overlooking Engels street, but the fourteen basement cells. That New Year's Eve she was fourteen in Emilija's mansion. Fireworks bombed the old town; the nation was independent! She drew close to read the shadow: pocked cement and a window blocked over with wood; the silent officer who asks no questions; the bucket; the brown sluice; the corridor; the faucet; the single shot; the ricochet's ring. Now her parents drink Black Balsam in the woods. The waiter grew old and went away to die. The night market is closed, she buys turnips under fluorescents at the Maxima. Her girls swirl out into the hot lights of the old town, they have law degrees and buy their clothes in Berlin. The trains run east, out of the city. She waits at the bar under the tiger's head, but Nyman left decades ago and her spine has curled to form a dromedary's hump, just as it did when he took her portrait, standing naked on the ladder to his lofty bed.

When the men in their red lapels and gleaming leather belts say "Come with us," they will bring her to the Corner House. And why has no one yet made a museum out of it? One plaque and the rest bombed out and boarded is insufficient. Shouldn't there be a list of names? The girls, one by one, are smitten: a backpacker from Ireland; an American student of medicine. They weep and laugh as they pack their things. One of the men in red lapels will be small-eyed, the other short and grinning. In the lobby of the Corner House, the summoned women will carry handbags and wear real pearls. At first, their voices will be outraged. Her apartment is iced and empty. In the west, Nyman's portraits of the gin girls, the soap girls, all the women off the city streets, gnaw the pine boards of their boxes and beg the locked doors not to open.

Record of Working

His physicists leave their idiot mistakes smeared across their tables, and during the night Arthur marks his corrections. In the morning nonconformity meetings they raise their insulted eyebrows—he has not sourced incompetents, they believe they can police themselves—but there are mossier issues: embedment plaques poxing the housing assembly; blue-sky disruption mitigation schemes from Garching and Palo Alto; lists of additions to the already-biblical ark of conductor metals. His team of design integrators are only four now, and every day at eighteen hundred hours the updates are re-disseminated with deviations flagged in green. At the workstations, bleary engineers take these changes, sometimes, as incidental.

Arthur, the first and only Director General of the project, chides grown men like a grade school math teacher. He stalks around in deep-pocketed camouflage trousers and an old Cambridge rowing blazer. The project is six years old. It is three years and nine months behind schedule. Every day of work costs into the millions: the precise number fluctuates, given the exchange rates on the thirteen different currencies involved, many of which are inflating hideously. Every few months the accountants come from their Domestic Agencies and sit behind their stiff little flags at the horseshoe dais in the glass-walled amphitheatre on Level 6. Up there they can look out over the entire compound: the reactor's seismic isolation pit populated by four hundred and ninety-three concrete plinths, the trailers, the machines, the debris. At night the military bathes everything in starry silver spotlights. In the centre of the pit, one hundred and sixty degrees of the ring fortress is black, hollow as a promise.

What Arthur has told them: to reach breakeven, plasma must stream—or drift, or sawtooth, or tear—in a four hundred second pulse. And then again, and again. One day it will be self-sustaining. The scale is critical. The Venezuelan Domestic Agency complains of the concrete shortage, but it's food shortages causing the riots. Of course it's severe. The forest is virginal. The sea eats the cliffs under colonial ruins. Energy will be delivered in milk bottles every morning. This was Arthur's vision and everyone understands that his visions come true. For instance, the Elemental Woman waits sleeping in his bed. And the sun achieved ignition, did it not?

Redout coughs and delays, but Arthur, who has never been later than forty-five seconds for anything, is absent. Ten minutes pass. Redout reads emails. Sunlight at this hour tracks across the blue jungle, but doesn't angle inside the room. The noise of the construction in the pit is muted, but given enough time it accretes in the skull, sludges the blood vessels. Every so often a concussion shivers his collar, and reminds him of other, lesser reactors that have failed: cataclysms even when they were the size of kitchen tables.

Greenhalgh and Boucher drain their coffees and scowl at the green scrawls on their schematics. Van der Meer types on his phone. Six others are wilfully late. Seventeen have cancelled their attendance on a temporary or permanent basis. It's May. The men who remain are wretched for a break.

"Clear enough?" says Redout. The appeal of impersonating Arthur's daily philippic is minimal. Boucher stretches and scratches his belly.

"All right," says Greenhalgh. He picks up his papers.

Van der Meer rises and walks out without lifting his eyes from his phone.

"Let's do it like this every day," says Boucher.

Redout dials Magda. Three rings in, he remembers the Elemental Woman and hangs up. He considers paging Arthur, but his nose wrinkles at the crudeness. The construction crews will pour the second segment of the ring fortress today; that is, the remaining two hundred degrees of the circle in which they will settle the torus' vacuum chamber, when it's built. An empty crown. Whenever that is—the components must be built, shipped, assembled. Years from now. A decade. The Haemorrhoid Pillow of Eternity, Boucher calls it. There can be no hollering for the Director General like a lost child at a supermarket.

Magda calls back immediately. Redout stares at his phone while it flashes.

"What is it?" she says.

"Oh. Hello, Magda. I'm sorry I hung up. I was afraid I'd bother you."

"Kind of you."

"You weren't sleeping?"

"Sleep?"

He chuckles. He grasps for a different question to ask her. The air stretches in one long, lordly parabola between them. Redout tucks his fist under his armpit. His voice is light. "I was just calling. I was wondering if you'd seen Arthur this morning."

"You haven't," she says.

"He's missed the noncon meeting, is why I'm asking."

"And why would you call me?"

"I know," he says. "I realize."

Magda's silence is dead and wooded. Eventually: "Ask her, then."

Redout clears his throat. "Indeed. Certainly. I will."

The line dies.

Again, he considers paging Arthur. The man has never carried a phone, but since construction began here five years ago he has also never been anywhere but headquarters and the house the Japanese Domestic Agency built for him on the cliffs, atop the ruins. To Redout's knowledge, he's never even left the compound.

From the descending glass elevator, the half-complete ring fortress is a cavity decked in orange flagging and red scaffolding. Yellow machines scuttle like wasps masticating their paper palace. The noise is wholly dissected from its makers—spasmodic, demonic—trucks spin their liquid rock and engineers shout. A fleet of agitators roils the concrete into all available crevices. They sound like doom approaching. The pour will continue for another nine hours. The practice pour last week was identical in every way, and the result sits over by the treeline, looking like a newborn gulag dropped from the clouds. The elevator doors open onto the empty lobby, where an infuriatingly fine white dust laps at the cement floor and clouds the hems of the glass walls.

For no good reason, the parking lot's grade is as geometrically immaculate as the reactor's basemat will be. There's no telling the Jeeps apart. Black boxes that rained down from the German Domestic Agency back when construction began. The lot is mostly empty because the military insists the construction crews bus in from the closest village, twenty kilometers away. There was a brief time when car engines were machinated into bombs. To spare himself squinting at every license plate, Greenhalgh has slapped a Manchester United sticker on the door of his Jeep. He used to cycle out to the village and back, until he was robbed the second time, less harmlessly than the first. Boucher's spray-painted a safety-orange peace sign on his rear window, and draped his side-mirrors with festive flagging like a child's tricycle. Boucher came from one of the failed tokamaks in Provence. Greenhalgh, meanwhile, came from fission, because fission is real and fusion only might be. In the beginning, it was easy to seduce the best minds to come devote themselves to this, the ultimate.

Right inside the military perimeter, where the local soldiers and their patriotic dogs make every morning a border crossing, Redout turns onto the dirt road that winds up the bluff. It's slippery. He used to feel some guilt over how the Jeep—which mutters of ecological and macroeconomic violence, war museums, bad television—is such a powerful comfort as compared to the exhaustless aluminum capsule in which he putted around Palo Alto. But, as they've learned, outside the perimeter the Jeeps are more than just a comfort. Soon there'll be no more hawing and they'll have to tighten belts and enlarge the living quarters for staff inside the perimeter, to house the construction crews. They will fall another year, two, behind schedule.

Arthur's house on the cliff is, like every building in the compound, made of glass. It's grown from the old stones of a Spanish fortress, as unlikely as a bright future. Certain bits of wood adorn rather than structure it. Ledges jut out over the ocean. The cliffs are granite and don't seem to be falling into the waves at any human pace, but the house is so sleek it looks like it could launch itself into orbit and escape all this suffering. Currently, the sun has flared it into phosphorous, white and silver. Arthur moved out in February, down into the coach house at the foot of the drive. Itself a dowdy offspring of its dam, blocked from the same genes and rubble. Built for one. Or two who want to be constantly entangled in each other. The Elemental Woman has lived there since she arrived.

Redout couldn't say which door he'd prefer to knock on right now. Magda's doubtless sitting alone in the cavern of the great room, swallowing a hundred miles of horizon in her glare. She has the kind of beauty the mind craves, and, partially because of this, when he met her his notion of certain realities became rearranged. But her field of warp extends only so far, and these days when he sees her the sky remains blue. It was good, in the end, that he'd never said anything to Arthur.

Redout pulls in at the coach house, behind Arthur's decaying station wagon, and the Elemental Woman descends a step from her doorway. Her hair is a black plasma of whorls, her hands are striped in burns. She is wrapped in sheer textiles, throat to wrist to ankle. He has seen her naked many times, as many times as he has seen her. She is standardly naked, or undressing, or re-dressing various parts of her contorting wireframe. Arthur, drunk, had stood and recited lines. He'd mouthed her fingers. That was the last time Magda had invited the executives for cocktails on the balcony. There had been dozens of them then. Now there are fewer, and none except Redout will visit Arthur at home.

"He's gone, if you're wondering." The Elemental Woman's lips are wide and raw.

"Where?" Redout lifts his hand against the sun.

Arthur calls her elemental. Part of his Working. But she was born Karen Barwick in Weston, Connecticut. The man she came here with was Italian, an electromagnetic engineer, but a replacement for him was soon found and he left quietly.

"How would I know?" she lifts and settles a piece of cloth over her shoulder.

"Did he leave a note? Say something?"

"You must think I'm extremely stupid."

"Of course I don't. I only wondered—"

"Talk to your government friends," she says. "They'll be able to find him. They'll want to kill him when they find out."

Redout has already stepped backward twice.

"Wouldn't it be easier for you if they'd just kidnapped him? That's probably what you should tell everyone, if you want to get out yourself."

"I have no idea," mumbles Redout, "what you mean." He opens his wallet, lifts out his card. "Would you call me if he contacts you?"

"He won't." She withdraws from his extended hand, folding into herself. She is beginning to look like women

137

do as they become useless. She is beginning to look terrifying. She steps back up into her house. Her voice is a lilt, a song: "I hope they catch him. I hope they burn him alive."

Magda watches Redout's truck slink back down the dirt track into the forest. From here, all she knows of the reactor is the occasional keen or drumbeat; it's invisible to her. Barwick's dollhouse is still. If Arthur is really gone then the woman is alone in there, turning from alien sink to alien bookshelf to alien bed. Potentially she is alive with agony. A current of emotion that can't be cut. Magda would tell her: one must wait until the generator runs down. One must have faith one will be left inert. There's no helping it. Whether a two-cylinder or a star. If it's a star, maybe, barbiturates. One must learn that being inert is the natural state. Magda has been titrating off the tranquilizers for three weeks now. She likes to lie on the balcony in the last of the sun with her herbs.

Three possibilities: one, Arthur has left, maybe with a woman yet-unknown; two, Arthur has died; three, Arthur is still in there and has Barwick playing some new game.

Because of the third possibility, Magda will not walk down the steps to the dollhouse to offer succour. There is a constant temptation to expose herself to new pain. Like dwelling in the memory of the two weeks that Arthur and Barwick spent in the master bedroom of this house while she lived here and Renata still lived here. She and Renata would drink tea in the autumnal January breeze and hear the animal sounds from the open windows. Ignore it like it was only the spider monkeys, the waves licking the ruins to dissolution.

Renata, eighteen by then, was grim. "Is this what I did to you?" she asked, once, as the fucking grew intolerable, the garden smell, the melodrama.

Magda palmed the girl's silky mermaid hair. "Of course not. You're my sister."

"Liar," said Renata. She had an instinct for self-preservation. She left within days. Wrote from Copenhagen that she'd paid her way in via shipping container. The girl spoke five languages. She'd found a job cleaning rooms. "You can come here!" she wrote. "No one's starving yet."

Another temptation towards pain: Magda still wears her wedding band. If she totals it up, week by week, she'd say she was happy for three months, all told. One month of those was ecstatic. It's been seven years since she met him, six and a half since she married him. She has seen the threshold of her tolerance. It is as wide and high as the horizon.

Immediately, Barwick finds that the house empty of him is so much more alive that breathing makes her giddy. She strips and burns linens and curtains. She opens windows and smashes the ones that won't. She avoids his rancid cave, cramped with the massive shrine of his work, except to throw every trace of him—books, clothing, papers—into it. Every day a ritual. He liked to tell her how he summoned her in there. A fortress of dirty objects. An insane person's altar to ego. He burned incense while chain-smoking and wore the same clothing every day without washing it or himself. He taped over the glass in every door and pinned the curtains to each other. He scribbled over the mirrors in black grease and stood, naked, staring into them, his fattening belly and soft penis. He starved himself and binged and shat. He read aloud to her from his daily writings and then locked his secrets away in a suitcase when he went to work on the reactor. His book, his Record of Working. Of course she read it, as the glamour of his genius dissipated in the stink.

You have had a result. The elemental. She is the perfect image in the heart of man, modelled by the awful lust in the space-time that forms all women, the insatiable and eternal. It vivifies the rose. Just as the little sister was used to effect transference of the weakness of the false woman's flesh to a critical period, just as your passion for the little sister also gave you the strength you needed at the time, confirmation of the Adultery and Incest in the Law, now the Elemental Woman has manifested in response to your call. The suspense and inquisition were your luck, you were enabled to prepare your thesis, formulate your will, take the Oath of the abyss and thus make it possible to manifest her in order to wean from wetnursing. She has demonstrated the nature of the woman in such unequivocal terms that you will have no further room for illusion on the subject.

He had her write, too, in a little notebook, her own record. Some days would rain dread as she tried to think of anything plausible enough to write down, knowing he would find it and read it. He'd scrawl in his corrections, steal whatever he liked as his own. He'd sneak out past the soldiers, who'd never been told how to recognize him. The phone would ring. "It's the President," he'd say. Arthur liked to orate to Barwick while he fucked her, an exposition of the women whose assholes and mouths he'd filled. He maintained an annotated list in his Record. Every time he fucked her, a new woman was described. The girl at the market who sold him incense; Van der Meer's wife; any scientist or bureaucrat who had come to work under him and been possessed of an adequate form; Magda, that poor crumbling statue of herself. Who else—Barwick smirked—who else had demonstrated *the nature* unequivocally? The stories had begun to overlap and entwine, if he were drunk or had been drunk or just lying. He had certain words and actions he'd go back to, when failing. When he came, he came in her because it was part of the Working. Their child would be born as the reactor was born, a god of eternal power. He'd never mentioned contraception. It seemed to never have occurred to him that she had control of that, that she could leave, that she could, living in all these dirty proofs, perceive him perfectly.

Magda's hypothesis is that the military perimeter will soon flex and invert and everyone within will be punished. The power still runs silently in her kitchen, but the food delivery is two days late. This is fine. She has always hoarded what she can. When they first arrived it was possible to drive into the village and buy sundries from the people in the market, though neither the women at the stands nor the soldiers with their dogs would deign to recognize her. Living as a ghost with him had been much lonelier than this current solitude. When she lived in Manhattan, before Arthur ensorcelled her, there were many men who knew her name. Here, she no longer needs one. Last year a famous American actress was murdered in her private villa. A college girl in Caracas was raped by nine soldiers. Now people gather where food used to be and scream at the soldiers and die. The violence, says the President, is due to the influence of television. The climate's drunk, liable to mania and then sullenness and then lashing out. Most herbs die, left on their own. She has to pay attention, bring the plants inside from the balcony every afternoon. Hail.

Magda used to buy her herbs from a girl who sold them in paper cups from her skeletal motorbike. The girl's ears jutted out under her cap. Her face, if cradled, would have rested against Magda's breast. Her nails were carved into dark, dim points like a badger's. She always smiled for Magda. She let Magda speak a little in Spanish. She said, "Do you know which you like?" Having a scrawny female to protect must motivate half the world's efforts. When Magda imagines what men must feel it makes her own missile body ridiculous. Tiny asses make cocks look big enough. Barwick, for instance, is narrow and contorted as a child. Magda lives constantly shocked by her own ugliness and beauty. She wonders every hour what she looks like: sea cow? Valkyrie? Her data points—beautiful, hideous—would blotch the grid to blackness. The famous actress was on holiday with her ex-husband and five-year-old daughter. How much suffering people tolerate, lingering where love used to be. Screaming for it. If she had brought the herb girl here to the glass ruin, she would've sucked the dirt from under her fingernails and lived off the momentum of that small thing's trust.

Again, her phone rings. Surely Redout, who's never said anything but "Of course" to Arthur. Instead, the soldier at the perimeter gate says, "I have a woman for you. Will you accept?" They drive her up. It isn't the herb girl with her friendly ears. This woman wears a backpack and a camera, like a tourist or a journalist, and a long braid. She hops the steps up to the door like she's been here many, many times.

"I summoned you!" Arthur had crowed, in front of everyone, while Barwick began to laugh.

The boy with the assault rifle at the compound's perimeter asks Redout to spell Arthur's name, as if he's never heard it before. And a second time. Then he shrugs. There is no record of Arthur leaving. Not coming, either, in the last five years, though yes, there he is on the list of residents, his photo faded out past recognition. Redout is unsurprised.

"Could a man go through the woods?" he asks. Beyond the razor-wire gate, the jungle swarms in still life, breezeless, embalmed in flowering vines. On this side, the air carries biting insects, and the sound of pouring rock.

The boy adjusts the rifle slung over his shoulder. "The dogs patrol all night."

It's eleven hundred hours. Redout must chair the weekly materials update. He goes back to the conference room on Level 4 as if he's spent the morning normally. Emails, coffee. Construction jitters the air. If they were on schedule, they'd be lowering the torus chamber, a flawless vessel fashioned from a single peel of material, into the housing by now. "The work is perfect!" Arthur always said. And yet, Redout never replied, the result is not.

Greenhalgh and Boucher are the only men in the conference room. It is all men on the project. Redout used to hire women in the beginning because they are cheaper and easier in so many ways, but Arthur ran through them like a wasting disease. He'd leave them useless, ruined for work, and then Redout would have to find a reason to send them away. They all went: docile or hissing, but they went.

"Droste says he needs another ten," says Greenhalgh.

"If we give him fifteen you think he'll find a way to stop the tungsten erosion?" Boucher spins in a slowing circle on his chair: legs crossed, hands raised like little wings. "Or will he just show us more slides of that Klimt painting with the nipples?"

"Maybe the nipples can absorb the thermal loads," says Greenhalgh.

"Droste is testing all sorts of pulse frequencies on those nipples. Those nipples are the hottest materials he's ever seen."

"Found Arthur yet?" says Greenhalgh. "Speaking of."

Redout pulls his gaze from the pit back into the room. "What do you mean?"

"You tell us," says Boucher.

Heat prickles Redout's neck inside his collar. He dials into the conference line with Droste in Garching, where the man's been bombarding monoblocks with neutron radiation for the last year and a half and sending back drawings of the little fissures he makes. The reactor will produce no waste, except for the reactor itself. The walls transmuted, the equipment irradiated. The problem is that there is no material invented yet from which to build the torus chamber. Even though the plasma itself will spin like a yolk inside an electromagnetic sac, everything melts at two hundred million degrees. Out in the void, uncontained, the sun's core burns tepidly at fifteen.

The conference line plays U2 while they wait.

Redout's phone flashes on the table. He picks it up. "A woman came," says the boy with the gun at the gate.

"Who?" says Redout.

"Cortez," says the boy.

"Who is she?"

"We drove her to the house. But now there is another. Dubois, she says."

"Just a second," he says. "I have to take care of this. Reschedule with Droste."

Greenhalgh lifts a hand. Boucher is spinning again.

"Do you know what she wants?" Redout asks the boy.

"The woman in the house."

"I want to talk to her first. Bring her here to me at headquarters. I'll meet you in the lobby."

There is a pause. "She says no."

"Send her here," says Redout.

The boy sighs.

Once, the real military came. They'd taken charge of the perimeter while the President visited. No one had understood that the gate guards weren't real soldiers until that day. Arthur's friendship with the President was close and long-standing, enough that—despite the Americans and Europeans—they had plotted together to build the reactor here, on this peninsula, where it would benefit them both first. Without Arthur there was no reactor. When the President had visited—toured the pit, sat behind his little flag on Level 6 during a woodenly optimistic diagnostics meeting—the gate boys had sulked around in their fatigues while the real soldiers manned every post.

Redout waits in the lobby, then the parking lot, but the boy doesn't bring any woman. They've ignored him. The Elemental Woman had said, "Talk to your government friends," but Redout is afraid. Droste's tungsten feathers like old bone. Arthur promised energy in milk bottles within ten years. Six hundred people once worked on this site daily, but that number has diminished as the coherence of the currencies drifts and families grow grey-faced behind barred doors at home. The thirteen Domestic Agencies supply fewer and fewer resources. There are wildfires in Austria and bread lines in Canada. It is difficult to ascertain at what point civilization has collapsed, because no one ever designated a quantitative measure, but Redout, if pressed, would say either they have thousands of years, or it's already over. Science will reveal all in the end. Superstition is the problem. Apocalyptic myths designed to scare people servile and meek. Women, whose bodies crack open like shellfish, who live for their naked infants, are so vulnerable to terror. Terror is what makes them humourless. They despair. They become murderous. Arthur, last month, drunk in his shrine at noon, held forth at volume: "God is the solar-phallic creative will, and the daughter is the virgin who unites with her father, stimulating him to reactivity and this begins the generative process all over again. This! This is what we're doing here. Four hundred seconds! It must be harsh! It's the scale of the thing!"

Redout finds his Jeep again and drives to the glass houses. In this last long, arid winter, amid all the other problems the project faced, Arthur began what he called his Working. Redout has seen the altar, yes. Redout was present as the seven verses were read aloud. Arthur naked and erect in a shroud of smoke. Redout had no choice but to record the proceedings, as requested.

Envision yourself a cloaked radiance desirable to her. As a man and as a god you have strewn about the heavens and earths many loves, these recall. Remember each woman you have ravished, think upon her, concentrate all into the Elemental Woman. Think upon your lewd Beast. Repent and recount your casual loves. Your lust belongs to her. Speak the Oath of the abyss. She is the Daughter of Fortitude, and ravished every hour from her youth. For behold, she is Rationality, and Science dwelleth in her; and the heavens oppress HER. She shall absorb thee, and thou shalt become living flame before she incarnates.

The door to the glass house is splayed. Bodies move against the aquarium sky, shadowed between windows. As he mounts the steps, another Jeep pulls up. Three women climb out. Their faces are familiar. A physicist, Van der Meer's wife, a woman from the village market. They don't glance at him as they file past him into the house.

Redout follows.

"I summoned you!" Arthur had crowed when they walked into his house one evening after work and found her standing there, smiling politely on the arm of the new poloidal-field-magnet engineer. Everyone heard Arthur say it. Men's wives, Magda, three quarters of the executive, Magda's young sister. Arthur took the woman's hand, kissed it like a king's. His face shone terribly. Tears fell from his eyes. "Finally. You've come," he said.

Inside, the women are in the kitchen, on the balcony, clustered in groups, buzzing around. Low laughter. At least two dozen of them. On a couch, one weeps into another's shoulder while a third—he recognizes the girl Renata, sixteen when she first arrived here—strokes her hair. Each woman he recognizes as one of Arthur's. Each one has giggled secretly with Arthur in an exhilarated dark. Women Redout himself has castigated or bribed or soothed, as their temperaments required. A lineage, a genealogy of women. They inculcate each other like exiles, reunited.

The glass walls are open to the ocean. The vibrato scent of newly fused ozone smashes up from the waves below.

Across the room, Magda fixes her gaze on him. Beside her, Barwick looks like a savage myth. Their faces are still. They have already summoned their solution, and ignited it.

A hand is placed on the nape of Redout's neck. Of course the reactor will fail. It already has. If it wasn't a fantasy, it was a nightmare. But he moved forward, didn't he? Is that not courage enough? In the face of it all, did he not do his work?

From above, the city lights are blocked black in irrational patches. The jet traces a descending compass curve. Skyscrapers are nothing but red pinpricks at their tips.

Whole districts are deleted. Buckled in his seat, Arthur ignores the burnt-up map below, scraping in his journal with his green pen.

—because of this test Rationality is incarnate upon the earth today, awaiting the proper hour for manifestation which was never NOW. The elemental was as false as any creature, all the squealing and manipulating that came before, she was no Daughter no vivification no result no IGNITION. This is proved in her infertile hole, though all men laboured upon it. Yea, you must strive abominable and be clothed with barncloth until you come into power and purple though you be contemptuous and solitary. Await the TRUE WOMAN who will flame the TRUE WORKING. Prepare yourself for portents. Prepare for the slaver of the hordes. Prepare all your priesthood and power—

His pen doesn't leave the paper he's scoring, not as the landing gear descends, not as the plane bumps against the tarmac. Finally, as the herd around him scrambles, he stuffs his papers into his rucksack and pushes his way out of the machine. He took nothing but the funds he had apportioned for his own needs. He sacrificed everything. But not everything! He will contact Andrea, or Elisabet. To continue his work, his reputation will require a salve of loving dedication. One of them, or both, must publish a piece exposing the superstitions and corruptions that crippled him.

He passes through border control with his new passport and hurries through the endless bright corridor towards a taxi that can take him to an appropriate hotel. A woman is walking towards him. She is young and beautiful. The corridor is empty. She meets his eyes, and he slows as she nears. She is clothed in a ravage of angelic light. The flame of her. He cannot help himself; he stops.

"Arthur," she says.

He's speechless. Did he summon her? Is she false? She is empty-handed, as if standing before her creator.

"Don't you know me?" she says.

"You?" Hope lights in him. The true, the ur. He is a boy. "Is it you?"

Her smile suffuses him with radiance. In the distance, thousands of kilometers behind him, he hears a monstrous concussion. So she rolled the beast down the street to this man, who is stocky and who jokes with his other customer, a kid who owns a sharp-featured Suzuki that's making, what, a bad sound?

La Folie

Nothing from the consul. At four, Audrey steps onto her balcony. The river's poured from the sky all day. All week. All three weeks, since she arrived. It falls onto then off of the hotel roof, and then into the river, which slithers the fore- and middle-ground both. No far side she's ever seen. She dismantles green oranges and stirs instant coffee, listens to the air conditioner choke, waits for the consul to call. Stay Hotel. Not that she has any other option. The water coalesces into sheets that slow time as they pass. Hunger keeps her shivering. Her slicker is cold, limp, vast: hammocking two chairs, dripping but never dry. She takes the third chair, square-cornered and shoddy. The neighbours' windows are propped open like the wet is good for them. The smoke will gather in their air, their linen, their decorative mosquito netting. She lights her cigarette. Foul.

Women don't smoke or drink here but she didn't smoke until she arrived. The truck driver offered her one of the nameless local things, and when she held it between her dirty nails she thought of Fawn. Fawn, who quits every September and starts again every December.

The neighbour's door squawks. The male of the two. He takes a stand on his own balcony, petite with baldish temples and wire-frame glasses. He does not say, *Bonjour, ça va?* as they all say to each other. He stretches his arms above his head and looks out into the airborne waters.

Now she's burnt up the cigarette's optimistic half. The dizziness happens. The stab of uplift. The stink lingers guiltily. The hotelier's flute starts up in the restaurant. She props her temple on her fingers. It sounds like several instruments. It sets the birdcages going. Further down the line, another man comes out, this one with his calfish daughter, brightly observing. More French. It's too late, the consul won't call now. From the balcony, the water falls back into the river. Catie will stay in her prison cell another night. In its dish, the cigarette dies without having transformed Audrey, or anything.

Things to do here are as follows: drink coffee with condensed milk on a low plastic chair; drink beer on a low plastic chair; walk past lines of docile, wicker-wrapped piglets; buy fruit and bitter nuts; watch what the mechanic will do to her motorbike; withdraw millions and millions from the bank machine; go to the soup woman; go to the rice woman; go to the grilled-meat woman and drop bits for the street dogs; go to the glass-doored minimart with the American chocolate bars and condom three-packs and imagine which breed she would buy, if she'd been the kind who got preferences.

At dawn, the bird in the cage beside her door renews its freedom campaign of sheer irritation. The rain mutters like news. It and hunger woke her again and again through the night. Today she'll get wet, as she's run out of toilet paper and won't ask the hotelier for more. She pinches her jeans where they hang: shades too dark.

She'd imagined beach, jungle, ruined temples, long boat trips up winding rivers. She'd feared the humidity. Tigers. The consul's office would be chilly and modern. The prison would be a horror. Catie would smile bravely, then dissolve in broken relief. That would take a day, at most three, then they'd take their bags to the resort where Catie had been living until the accident. La Folie Douce. They would learn about each other. She'd imagined Catie's gratitude. Catie's advice. Catie's generosity. How they'd stay for a long time, months maybe, like that. Audrey has so many questions. Audrey has not seen her sister since she was five, which was twenty-five years and eleven weeks ago. The prison, the consul told her and her parents, is forbidden to foreigners. There isn't even an address. No.

Is it the hunger or the rain that makes it impossible to walk the path to the hotel restaurant? Audrey lingers on her balcony, aware of a rational mind but unable to access it. Her neighbours are able. They sing-song their civil language. The women wear loose trousers with bright prints, press their hands prayerfully in greeting and issue negligent commands. She cannot eat with them. These humiliating people. While walking towards them she walks past and through the sopping garden and out into the street.

Motorbikes carry duos, trios, of plastic-cowled commuters. Their wheels reverse the rain; drench ankle and knee. At night, mototaxis strafe the French men, drivers cooing, "Marijuana? Ladies? Marijuana?" They ignore her. Audrey lights another unconscionable cigarette. Burnt butcher offal. War latrine. The pack cost fifteen thousand. A wet dog squints from beneath the awning of the store-front across the street. She's old, sucked out, bedizened with dangling tits. Beside her, men are constructing a build-ing using a scaffolding of slender tree trunks. They've lit fluorescents against the dim. Her gut squirrels inside itself. Her toes spoon up silt. A block away, the rice woman nods as Audrey squirms out of her plastic sheet. The only other customer is a man hunched into his noisy phone.

Catie's island resort is a few miles up the coast. Audrey passed signs for it on her way down from the city. Her motorbike, when she bought it, came outfitted with new tires and brakes, and the assurances of the dealer, who employed young European men to coddle and persuade customers like her. Neither odometer nor speedometer functioned. The fuel gauge only partially. They're not supposed to work, she was assured. She'd putted along the edge of the broad new highway, buzzed by trucks and better bikes, the clouds descending by the kilometre. Here, the hotels are full and the French walk around with elaborate camera bulges. She is told that on the other side of the river the bullet holes haven't been patched in the walls of the royal citadel. There are waterfalls. If there were tigers, they died in the wars.

A child, unfamiliar with walking, clings to the rice woman. She delivers to Audrey a plate of knucklebones and tangled garlic weeds. The child stares. Her hair falls from a hopeless tail. Her fist deposits a crumpled blue bill on Audrey's lap. Two thousand.

"Oh no!" says Audrey, and pushes it at the rice woman, who plucks it back without looking.

Audrey eats what's possible of her meal. She tries to imagine a thing to do next. A reason to stand. To continue.

She picks through her fistful of cash. The woman nods as she approaches the necessary amount.

"Here," says Audrey, proffering another of the worthless blue bills, "For your little girl."

The child turns her face away. The woman says a word and the child allows one eye to peer.

Audrey laughs brightly. She puts the bill on the closest level surface, where the meat is cut. Both woman and child ignore it. She has eaten here a dozen times and doesn't know the woman's name or what the meal is called. She just sits, and a plate is passed. She cools her blush re-entering the slimed blue tunnel of her slicker. No, no. That was a mistake. Now she can't come back here. The places where her money is worth taking keep dwindling. Last week a woman failed for ten silent minutes to notice that she wanted to buy a squat hand of bananas. Audrey can't see clearly in the glare off her own effort. She is always paying with what isn't hers.

The duties she performed were as follows: wake Fawn in the morning, once or twice; make Fawn's bed; cheerlead Fawn's morning plyometrics; coerce hydration; enjoin Fawn to feed or pet the dog; attend to Fawn's self-directed endeavours; launder textiles; ensure healthful and calorically appropriate food intake; maintain vigilance against descending or chaotic emotional weather; iron and fold or hang textiles; supervise macro- and micro-task list and supply appropriate reminders and encouragements; suppress emotion convincingly; listen actively; monitor and supplement physical appearances, both Fawn's and her own; attend all events, formally sanctioned or not; chaperone all foreign males, especially offsite, especially in-room; offer good counsel; soothe; stroke; murmur; hold through quivering; listen to wailing; report developing concerns; fuel the creation of personal narratives and mythology; build capacity for empathy, willpower, humour, and self-esteem; remain sober and watchful through binges; exercise, feed, and pet the dog; turn down the bed; fetch water; wake and answer calls in the night when nightmares soak the sheets with sweat; change them.

The third mechanic wears rubber flip-flops and squats yogicly as he wrenches at her engine's viscera. Washers skitter the cement. Her motorbike, she knows now, is not even a Honda, but a knock-off from China. The cube with aortal valves is the carburetor. The fingerling in the wheel well is a spark plug. The problem is that it won't start, or it won't start without gas, or it won't start unless the idle mix is enriched via screwdriver, or it won't start in the rain, and that when it finally starts it stalls at low speeds, and even if it doesn't stall, turning the key won't turn it off, the gas must be choked via a toggle deep in the beast's phlegmatic chest. The third mechanic is rewiring an electric jugular related, it seems, to one of these problems, none of which Audrey is able to name in any language.

She sits, alert, on a red plastic chair, knees to tits. She wears her slicker because the awning drips. The kickstarter bruised her ankles. Today she tried to turn the engine over. On first attempt it sounded close, but she didn't rev it hard enough and by the fifth, sixth attempt, it was impossible. Something inside rattled. The French pretended not to see her distress. So she rolled the beast down the street to this man, who is stocky and who jokes with his other customer, a kid who owns a sharp-featured Suzuki that's making, what, a bad sound? "Tktktktktktk," says the kid. Audrey wishes her problem had a sound. She pokes at her phone and tries to make it translate her questions: *Is it the battery? Is it the rain?*

The third mechanic's shop is the patch of sidewalk in front of his living room. Exhaust fills the air not occupied by dripping water. The living room is white tile with a carved wooden sofa decked in blankets. A boy, the son, negotiates videos on a large flatscreen.

A teenage girl arrives on a pink bicycle. Her flip-flops are dirty white. CHANNEL, they read. The mechanic says some words to her without gesturing at Audrey. The girl turns. "Didn't you check the engine before you bought it?"

"I don't know anything about engines. I just trusted him." She tries to laugh, but her voice is strained high.

With a flick, the girl transfers her slicker from her shoulders to the handlebars of her propped steed. The mechanic says something else. She says, "He says you need a new carburetor."

"Okay," says Audrey.

"Two hundred and fifty thousand," says the girl.

"Wonderful," says Audrey. "Perfect."

The girl goes inside to her brother and touches his head. The mechanic begins a second wave of deconstruction. The girl returns, chewing.

"Where are you from?" she says.

"America," Audrey generalizes.

"How long you staying?"

"I'm not sure," says Audrey.

"Not sure? What's your job?"

Audrey doesn't hesitate. "I'm a junior partner at a law firm."

"A lawyer?"

"Yes," Audrey lies. There's no serviceable word for what she was. The bank categorizes such agreements as *debt bonds* and the government legalized them under the *International Family Futures Act*, but in the executed document she was merely the *Second Party*, her name a note beneath her mother and father's authorizations. Not chattel, not a serf or a servant or a drudge. Fawn's trust was the *First Party*. Not Fawn, Fawn always reminded her. Fawn's trust.

The girl grunts. "So you like rain a lot?"

"It's beautiful," Audrey lies again.

The girl laughs. "Your husband likes rain?"

"No husband," says Audrey. "Yet."

The girl snickers.

"And my sister," says Audrey. "My sister likes it here. What's your name?"

"Thu," says the girl. She presses buttons on her cracked and sparkling phone. "Add me as a friend."

"I don't have that," says Audrey.

"Why not?"

Audrey shrugs, twists her hand in the way people here do when they mean *give up, go away, don't make me explain.* She says, instead: "Your English is very good."

"My mother teaches it," says Thu. "I take her classes. My international name is Jessica Margaret." She flashes the screen: a sultry selfie and a gaggle of girls by a lake.

"My name is Audrey," says Audrey.

"Look." Thu butts her shoulder against Audrey's and angles downward. On the screen: a pretty girl attended by a cringing one.

When Audrey returned to her parents' house the day after her thirtieth birthday, the days went as follows: wake up in Catie's peach-sheeted virginal bed, to which Catie herself has never returned, even for a night; examine Catie's adolescent trove of educational materials and electronic obsoletes; hover at the stairtop, tuned for signs of life below, and, if none, descend to forage coffee and toast; read handy texts—fat series of popular novels, news feeds, aspirational magazines—until startled by car noise, mail delivery, or other reminders of external life; wash in a bathroom populated by store-brand serums; dress in clothes that looked paltry under Fawn and ludicrous here, which are often Fawn's own clothes, or knock-off versions of what Fawn might wear; walk into town, fifteen minutes along unswept asphalt and over the slime-rocked river; note Help Wanted signs while skirting the pharmacy where her mother tends cash and the gas station where her father manages unkempt young men who flirt with any females who can afford to drive cars despite the price and dearth of the products that formerly constituted the ecstatic fortune of this region, this town; eat a day-old pastry at the coffee shop; read more: usually local flyers, abandoned paperbacks; walk back to the empty house; tidy it; array Red River College legal-assistant distance-education materials convincingly; forage more calories; work silently as mother sheds uniform, pours rum and coke, heats dinner; work silently as father enters, cracks and carries beer can to recliner in front of TV news; ensure contribution of minimum three sentences while eating the meal; wash dishes; ghost upstairs to virgin bed. If, on any day, either parent remained at home, Audrey lingered in Catie's room, if not her bed, indefinitely.

Her phone refuses to access information via any of the usual processes. The screen freewheels joyously. Audrey walks to the hotel restaurant and, dripping, keeps pushing buttons.

The hotelier approaches with a menu. The food is not good. Wet eggs and stale bread every morning, coffee sick with sweetener: all this for fifty-five thousand. The good breakfast is soup, but that would require rising at six a.m., walking down the block to the soup woman, scouting an empty stool among the cramped tables, waiting meekly to be noticed. Waiting for a while. Last time, Audrey imagined resentment. Not just the soup woman's, but the soup eaters', and she crumpled inward, and waited some more, and the soup didn't come, and finally she left. Now she can't go back. She must eat the bad baguettes.

"My phone won't work," she says.

The hotelier is both taller and thinner than she is. He wears a red-and-yellow striped soccer jersey and the same genus of wire-framed spectacles as his guests. "Your phone," he says.

"*Ne marche pas*," she says. She pushes it at him so he can translate the ominous, incomprehensible messages she's been receiving from the phone company.

He shakes his head, maybe sympathetically. "It won't work," he explains.

"I know," she says. "Do I have to get a new one? A new card?"

"Yes, a new one," he says.

"But I'm waiting for a call from the consulate," she says.

His eyes drift at the soprano note of woe. The French are listening.

"I need to use your phone. So the consulate can call me back here. And you can tell me. Okay?"

The hotelier lifts his hand as if to wave her off, but instead he manifests a corded plastic handset, and allows the number to be read aloud from a business card. Audrey listens at the little holes. A recorded voice speaks.

She says to it, "Hello, it's Audrey Coy? My sister is Catherine Coy? My phone is broken so if you could please call my hotel with any news. I've been waiting? It's been three weeks since you said—since she was supposed to be released. When can I see her? Can you just? Can you call me?"

She hangs up, and then she calls back and leaves the hotel's number.

The French are paying their bills, quietly. A little girl is arguing with a brother, who snivels. The young mother—very young, especially in comparison with the balding father—ignores them, her thighs crossed in royal-blue clown pants. Audrey, in the front garden, notes that the construction across the street has progressed. Now the tree trunks support a newborn slab of concrete. She must fix her phone, and she must eat, and she must check whether her motorbike will start today: its temperament changes by the hour. It has or is a chronic illness, a heartbreak, a blade that bleeds her every time she forgets and remembers again.

She walks past a pastry shop—a soapy glass counter with plastic chairs in front—where Thu is sitting with other girls.

"Thu!" Audrey calls.

Thu's hair is plaited in fishtails. Poppy-orange lipstick makes her look serious. She's the prettiest of her friends. They pick at beignets.

"My hotel is right there," Audrey hops over, smiling, realizing she has nothing to say. She points to the beignets. "What are those? Are they good?"

A new beignet is fetched from the display and presented in a scrap of wax paper.

"Oh, wow. Thank you! Thanks," Audrey sits down in the empty chair nudged wide. "How much? I can pay."

Her wallet is ignored. The other girls murmur to each other over their phones.

"Why aren't you guys in school?" Audrey smudges her fingers into the wet sugar.

"Today is a study day for senior students," says Thu.

The beignet is bread filled with custard, but the flakes on top are salted and fishy. Now Audrey is afraid this is not Thu, that she has mistaken this girl for Thu, and the girl is just being polite to an idiot. But no, her eyebrows are long and sharp like Thu's. The pink bicycle stands in the gutter stream, and the CHANNEL flip-flops are dirty and white.

"What are you studying?" says Audrey.

"I.T." says Thu.

Thu's friends don't meet eyes, though Audrey sends little glances and smiles. She wipes her lips. Fish flakes melt away in the eternal waterfall of her slicker.

"I have a question. Maybe you can help me?" Audrey pulls out her phone. "It stopped working."

Thu regards the messages for a grim second. "It's blocked. Buy a new card."

"I just bought this one. Two weeks ago."

Thu shrugs.

"Where should I go?"

"Anywhere," Thu says. She twists her hand, like, *I can't use your eyes for you.*

"Is there a store close?"

"Yes," says Thu.

The friends are silent, staring off into the street as the sugar dilutes in their blood. When she was with Fawn, every finished moment required a fresh anticipation.

Future pleasure. Audrey places her gutted beignet respectfully on the table and produces her pack of terrible cigarettes. "Thank you for helping," she says. She lights one, saying, "Sorry. Thank you. That's very helpful."

Thu watches her mouth. The smoke flees up into the awning, drifts. Fawn used to blow smoke rings. She'd lean her head back and work her jaw like a constrictor. Loops disintegrating. It's unbearable, how long time lasts. Thu blinks.

"Do you want one?" says Audrey.

A girl titters, and Thu picks one out of the pack with her glossed nails. She glances up.

"Put it in your mouth," Audrey reminds her, lifting the lighter. Flinch of embarrassment. The friends' taut attention. Thu tilts her head back and exhales. Perfect, wealthy languor.

"Terrible," says Audrey.

"Very, very bad," says Thu.

Catie spent the proceeds of Audrey's twenty-five-year bond as follows: four years in private middle school; four years in boarding school; four years in an undergraduate double honours degree in economics and political science; three years in law school, including eight months of internship; one year as a junior commercial lending associate; two years as an insurance defense litigator; five years as a senior litigation associate; one year and nine months as a non-equity junior partner; a few months living on an island whose name her family didn't know until the phone call came from the consulate. One hundred thousand, is what that cost. Almost eleven dollars a day. A few weeks after Audrey flew from LAX to YEG and then caught a four-hour Greyhound northwest to the town where she was born and where her parents still lived, Catie was arrested. A few weeks after that, Audrey flew here.

In the bathroom Audrey's left sock soaks up a puddle. Above, the gypsum distends, cystic, around the light bulb. She swallows her salt toothpaste and combs her greasy bangs behind her ears. She listens at her own door before opening it. How simple to wait until a room of French—the small family, the blonde mother and daughter, the loud old man—roll their bags away and then slip inside the abandoned room. She steals a bottle of water, a roll of toilet paper, and a chocolate bar. One mattress has a smush of old blood: a rolled-upon mosquito. As she mouses back to her own room, a girl in a hospital mask and apron comes around the corner. Audrey jerks into a smile.

"May I clean?" says the girl.

"There's a leak!" Audrey pins the chocolate bar against her thigh. "In the ceiling! I'll show you!"

The girl ducks through Audrey's damp web of hung items, eyes the sagging ceiling, then empties the trash. She fetches new towels from her cart. Audrey proffers the dirty coffee mug, and glass, and teaspoon, which the girl accepts and carries to the bathroom sink, where she washes them with the tiny bar of hand soap. Audrey seats herself in shame on her crumpled sheets.

"More water?" The girl sets a fat roll of toilet paper on top of the dusty television.

"Thank you so much!" Audrey sounds terrified to herself. "Wow, thank you!"

The girl nods, and goes along to knock on the next door.

What is the punishment for stealing a chocolate bar? It's not certain that the girl noticed, but how could she have not? Audrey wings her wet mantle over herself and goes to the hotelier in the restaurant. "There's a leak in my room," she tells him. "Rain is coming through the ceiling."

The hotelier nods. "Okay," he says.

"In the bathroom," she says. She thought she'd try to pay for the chocolate bar but the words don't sound. She sets her key on the table before him. "I'm going out but I'll be back. Has anyone called for me?" "No calls," he says.

"Okay," she says.

"Excuse me," he calls. She stops on the gravel path. He grimaces. "How long will you stay?"

"Stay?" she says. "I don't know. I wasn't planning, really. I'm waiting for a phone call. You know." She mimes the phone.

He shows her a pad of pink paper—*Facture*. "Twenty-eight nights." He slides his pen down the dates. The total at the bottom is 18,200,000.

Audrey's throat closes.

"Twenty-eight nights," says the hotelier again. He told her his name the first day, but she forgot it immediately. Other guests use it. They all joke around in French, which he also speaks.

"Yes, but," Audrey says. She tries to do the math. The daily rate written is 650,000. She points to it. "I thought you said six."

"Yes, six for the room, six fifty if you use the air conditioner."

"But it's cold out!" she says. "I only turn it on for white noise. To sleep! I would've used the fan. You didn't tell me!" Her voice quivers.

The hotelier tilts his head as the annoying bird adds its own shrieks. Maybe he told her. Maybe she remembers him saying something like that when she'd first arrived soaked and starving in a truck with her syncopetic motorbike in the back, after two hours weeping at a gas station on the highway, watching a man who may or may not have been a mechanic examine her bike, run it, watch it die again. She'd paid the driver 1,000,000 to carry her the last thirty-six kilometres into town. No English, no French. Tears drizzling her face steady as outside. The truck driver had offered her that first cigarette. He'd also offered tissues, which made her sob harder. The rooms had looked so warm and dry, the balcony so promising: perfect, once the weather cleared.

"Okay," the hotelier flaps his hand calmingly. He punches at his calculator. 17,000,000.

"I have to go to the bank," Audrey says. "I have to check out."

"Okay," he says. His eyes slide away to fix on something easier.

As she walks, muddy-ankled under her cowl, to the ATM, a motorbike skates through puddles alongside her.

"Hey!" says the driver. "Where you from?" He is young, with long, bare calves and golden flip-flops.

"America," says Audrey. "Actually, no. That's not true. I'm from Whitecourt, Alberta."

"You're very beautiful."

"Yeah, okay," says Audrey.

"Where are you going? You want a tour?"

"I can't afford a tour. I'm poor."

"Tour of the citadel? Tour of the waterfall?"

"Marijuana?" says Audrey. "Ladies? What about a husband? Can I have a husband?"

The driver stops, puts his foot down in the gutter stream. He is her age, lean and handsome. She scuttles away, into the ATM's plexiglass box. The maximum withdrawal is three million. She dips the card six times, relieved and disturbed that this abuse doesn't block the account. Her parents' account. Her parents' money, which is not plentiful, which is Catie's money, transferred monthly. She needs Catie. Catie's credit score, Catie's social score. Catie's slenderness, Catie's condo in Dumbo, Catie's casual raw silk, Catie's glassy intelligence, Catie's eyelashes, Catie's tutors, Catie's willpower, Catie's early-morning meditation, Catie's metabolism, Catie's aura, Catie's fate. She'd believed, she believes, that if she gets close enough to it, somehow—well. She has held so much hope in the vessel of herself. Hope flutters against the glass, beating the same choreography as fear. Identical aliens. Just imagine something better and you'll fear losing it.

Audrey peers outside through the condensation smear. The taxi driver has moved on. Walking back to the hotel, she sees a display of smuggled cigarettes among the stacks of flip-flops, plastic baskets, and clown pants. Marlboro, Marlboro Gold, three colours of Camels. She selects one of each: 225,000 total. "Fuck it," she grins at the woman, who gazes at her unwieldy fold of new bills. "Right?"

Outside the shop, under another awning, she lights one. The taste is still so bad. Fake, then. Okay. Also fake.

Things that Fawn has written since Audrey left are as follows: *I keep dreaming you're leaving and waking up and you're gone; I'm sorry, I'm crying again; I don't know how to handle this without you; You must think I'm so pathetic with my pathetic problems; I can't even understand what's going on*

in your head right now, where you are, what you're thinking;
Do you hate me?; Just tell me you're okay; Just write me back;
I'm so sorry; Was this ever real to you? Did I know you? Did
you always hate me?; Did you hate me more when I knew than
when I didn't?; I swear to god it was so real to me; You're the
only real thing that's ever happened to me; I don't know who I
am without you; You can't blame me for this; Stop punishing
me; The money isn't me; What would I have to pay you to
come back?; This silence is inhumane, it's abusive; I know your
parents' number and I will call them if you don't tell me you're
okay; I'm so fucking sorry, Aud; This makes no sense; Please
just come back; Please just forgive me; It's not my fault.

Chickens run like thoughts in the street while Audrey putts
around in the mud. Her bag is corseted to her bike with
neon cords. All the hotels are full up. It's the high season,
this downpour. Her bike is stalling again, which means it
will cease to start soon. She parks at a guesthouse that is
tiers of private karaoke rooms, and then, an afterthought,
a line of sleeping rooms at the back. Men drink iced beer
in a white tile courtyard where a dog sleeps in a cushioned
wicker chair. The room the woman shows her is also white
tile, both walls and floor. The sheets are teddy bears saying
Love! There is one fuzzy red blanket on each twin bed. A
red light is taped to the wall between them, a yellowing
cord snakes down. The opaque window, muscled open,
overlooks a dripping green slough. She shuts it immediately against malaria.

"The karaoke is not that loud," the woman says.

"Isn't there a bathroom?"

"The lobby."

"How much?" says Audrey.

"For one night, one fifty."

"Fine," says Audrey.

"Now," says the woman.

"Fine," says Audrey, pulling bills from her remaining slip of funds. "Why not."

"How long will you stay?"

Audrey's chest closes. She shrugs and twists her hand, like, *how could one ever possibly want to leave this heavenly palace?* Finally, the woman walks away, leaving the key in the door. Audrey's bag squelches froggily on the spare bed.

She drives her bike back to the mechanic, and stands beside it in the rain until he comes out of his living room. "It's broken again," she says.

He looks at it.

"Can't you just swap the spark plug or something?"

He looks at her.

She raises her voice. "Spark? Plug?"

The sun has apparently set. The rain has blackened. Inside his house, there's video noise and the smell of a complicated dinner. He waves his hand in the negative. *Neither you nor your machine.*

"Fine. I'll come back tomorrow." She drops the kickstand. "I don't care."

He doesn't make her move it, which is good enough.

Audrey heads back up the street, rain weeping down her neck, spine curdled against it. Here is Thu, shuffling home under an umbrella, wearing a long green dress. Strappy plastic heels dangle from her purse.

"Hello!" says Thu. "How are you, Audrey?"

Audrey's face must be itself because Thu's smile wavers.

"Not good," says Audrey. "Bad."

"Oh no. Is it your awful motorbike?"

"It's my awful motorbike," mocks Audrey.

"I'm so sorry for you." Thu even looks sorry. What does she want? A cigarette?

"Why are you all dressed up?"

Thu straightens, brushes a hand down silk. The green is a breed of sportswear neon: firefly. Slits up the side to her hips, elegant black trousers underneath. Still, CHANNEL. "It's portrait day for senior students. At the citadel."

"In the rain? With the bullet holes?"

Thu shrugs.

"Awesome," Audrey mutters. She dips her hand inside her slicker for her cigarettes. "Want one?"

Thu's eyes shift up the street to the mechanic's.

"Worried dad will be mad?" Audrey snorts. "Come see my new hotel then. It's a dive. They don't give a fuck."

Thu narrows her eyes. "Sure," she says, mispronouncing the word.

The tile courtyard is lit like a public bathroom. Tinnitus yowls filter from the karaoke rooms, all of which are marked VIP. Men wear soccer jerseys over their potbellies and cluster around tables with purpose. The woman brings a single large, warm bottle of beer, a bucket of ice with tongs, and one glass mug.

"Excuse me," says Audrey, "One more glass?"

The woman doesn't hear. Audrey digs up the fake Marlboro Golds. For a moment, it feels like a celebration. "These are much better than that shit yesterday, oh my god." Her voice sounds like Fawn's.

Thu takes discreet sips, talking about her friends and her IT exam and her aunt in Australia. She leans back in her seat and closes her eyes. Audrey twists around, lifts her hand twice, and finally goes into the lobby to fetch another bottle of beer. She collects three, because the woman is obviously too busy to do it herself.

A man is hollering at Thu. One hand is waving tentacularly over his private cemetery of beer bottles. Thu is pivoted in her seat, snicking retorts, hackles up. Audrey glares as she approaches. She touches Thu's shoulder. The man throws his arms up as if vindicated.

"Let's go inside," Audrey says, instead of asking. "Fuck these gross old drunks."

Thu takes the cloudy mug off the table and follows. "I hate—" she says, but doesn't finish the thought. She inspects the teddy bear sheets, the red light. Audrey's pathetic home.

"Isn't this the literal worst?" Audrey declares as she bolts the door behind them. Fawn's voice. Fawn. "Total fuck shack."

"Why are you here?" says Thu.

Audrey pretends to not hear the question, hands the girl her own new bottle of beer. "Do you know that guy? What was he even saying?"

"Always the same old stupid man," Thu says. "I wish I left tomorrow."

"Where are you going?"

"University. I have to go to Ho Chi Minh City, but I should go to Singapore. I was accepted to Singapore. It's too much money."

"Maybe you can transfer. You know, later. Get a scholarship."

"What scholarship?" Thu laughs like this is a thing the drunk man has said. "Where did you study?"

"Nowhere," says Audrey.

"What?" says Thu. "You said lawyer."

Audrey shrugs as if Thu misunderstood. "My sister is a lawyer. She went to all sorts of private schools and American colleges. I paid for it. I did a twenty-five-year debt bond."

"Your parents sold you?"

Audrey shrugs again. "She was just better than me. She scored better."

"I would kill myself."

"I was five. I went to California. There was a little girl, Fawn. I was supposed to teach her responsibility. Like a dog."

"That's shit," Thu unfolds on the bed. A wrist blocks the ugly light from her eyes. "My parents think I am eating dinner with my friends. But they are all with their boyfriends."

Audrey opens another bottle. "Where's your boyfriend?"

"I don't want one."

"I want one," says Audrey.

"So now your sister is a big lawyer."

"She quit her job. She lives here now." The half-truth falls out, unexamined. The better half of reality. "Up the coast? La Folie Douce? I'm going to meet her there soon."

"She'll give you money?"

"No. Maybe. It's her money."

"What will you do with it?"

"I don't know."

Thu snorts. "You can make a scholarship. Can I have another cigarette?"

Audrey extracts one, rather than passing the pack. "Better go outside," she says. Fawn was the one who gloved her imperatives in innocence, to a point.

Thu flicks the lighter twice, toes her flip-flops.

Audrey picks up her phone and fusses with the Wi-Fi. The password is printed on a piece of paper taped to the wall. She never bought another SIM card, she remembers. She remembers the consul. He could've called the old hotel. Catie could be waiting, withered in grey rags, in his office right now, ready to take her life back. Will she even care that Audrey came for her? That she's waited all these weeks? Catie never said anything. In twenty-five years not a note or a phone call. Audrey has to find a phone. She stands up.

Thu is not outside. The men are standing swayingly. The doors to the VIP rooms are open, and competing cacophonies blare out in flashing colours, but no one is singing. Some are shouldering into windbreakers, examining wallets. Audrey narrowly remembers to take off her shoes as she enters the lobby, edges past the family's living room. At the desk, three officers in beige uniforms, two in green, are speaking to the woman. Another waits outside by his fat-haunched motorbike. The officer Thu is squeaking at is not listening, but waving her silent: *shut up, it's useless, you're no one.*

Audrey turns around.

In her room she picks up her sopping bag, tucks her phone in her backpack, and skitters around the corner of the building. A muddy path skirts the slough and she follows it, tripping in trash, until it swerves back onto the street. Her slicker is still draped wetly in her room, but the rain is as light as it ever gets. Like it's on the verge of retraction, regret. Her bike is still standing in front of the mechanic's house, heading a row of half-cannibalized skeletons. She knocks mirrors and rocks kickstands as she rolls it away. The police will call him. He'll go retrieve Thu. Take responsibility for what she's done. Something explicable. It is lewd to show affection in public, she read. It is illegal for a foreigner and a national to cohabitate in a hotel without a marriage contract. It is disrespectful to touch another person's head, even a child's. No tank tops. Thu must be at least seventeen. Was it the smoking or the beer? It can't have been the room. What is the legal age here? The legal age for a girl? Was it because she was rude to the woman? Or was it because the men were drunk, and because the hotel was shitty and they were poor and aging bitterly? Did Catie feel so ignorant? What did she say when the witnesses crowded her and her carnage, gaping at what she'd done?

Audrey inserts the key, presses the button, twists the throttle so brutally that the engine resurrects itself with damning noise, as if it had been suffering badly, in silence, for too long.

Catie's days on the island passed as follows: a rush out of tense, watery dreams, guided by the Jurassic call-and-response of roosters in the charcoal-filtered dawn; group meditation on cushions; a floral tea on her stilt porch in the face of the Cyclopean sun as it launched out of the gulf's cloudbank; then a jog around the perimeter through the narrow, steaming paths, dodging motorbikes and water buffalo and snotty, bitten dogs; breakfast of tangy bananas on toothpicks affixed invisibly with unopened buds at their tips; English conversation at the primary school with the children in their navy skirts and trousers; lunch of soup, noodles, and chicken bones; an excursion via motorbike to see the dolphins, or a hike to the temple at the top of the hill, or possibly even a swim at the waterfalls from a boat with a long-tail engine dipping into the wake like a dragonfly's abdomen; maybe a nap or quiet sex under the mosquito netting; some reading of the German and French paperbacks left in little wooden libraries all over the village; evening meditation, solo; a quick jaunt to the inland shore for a gin from her private bottle or a glass of good red wine as the clouds exploded in lionish, gleaming tatters over the western archipelago and the blue fishing boats; back at the resort, in the purest black, fresh fruit and rice for dinner with a large bottle of cold water, while she thought she could never get bored of this life, while she thought she would never go back, not for anyone, not for any reason she could imagine.

The rain needles Audrey's eyes and smears the asphalt sideways. Without her slicker she's shuddering and crone-clawed in a bad wind. Her speedometer still doesn't work, but she can't be going faster than thirty-five. She pulls her feet up into the spinal dip of her beast, away from the tires' wake, and curls over them to shelter at least a dream of core warmth. She aims north, slowing to peer at signs, paranoid. The rain splinters the black to a worse black. This takes hours. Has she missed it? She passes the gas station where the truck driver twisted his fists under his eyes to cheer or mock her before he rolled her dead bike onto his truck. Her headlight is dim. Her joints are locked. Her jaw clatters. Her heart has a pain in it when she remembers how, last time, her bike just slowed, slowed, stopped. But it keeps shuddering on in its own stream. The black thins, maybe. The turn-off is a mud road, potholed and flooded. Something clanks darkly under her left knee. Trees, wooden shacks, dogs like corpses. Even if the consul had told her where the prison was, she wouldn't go. She never even wanted to.

The road ends with a mudslide into the grey pull of water. Across, there: the island, a line of red burning behind starburst palms. A fat young woman wearing a floral windbreaker and a conical hat is sitting in a pencil of a wooden boat. She looks up from her phone when Audrey says, "Ferry?" The woman pushes a wooden pallet into the water.

Audrey's hands are so cold she can't unfurl them, so she can't twist the throttle or pull the front brake properly. The ramp doesn't even reach the shore, she'll have to dip into the water to use it. The bike will slide in the mud. She might gun it too hard and jolt over the boat, into the waves. The boat, which looks like it was made from a leaf. She exhales. She goes. Zips down the bank and up the ramp in a neat swing. She laughs as she drops the kickstand and kills the engine. "Oh my god," she keeps saying. The woman waves a hand: *sit down, lady*.

The water is lax. The sky opens up in mounds of mauve and saffron. The boat's engine churns against crowds of little wavelets. They pass lush clumps of greenery, possibly tethered, possibly roving. Audrey puts her hands under her shirt. Her belly is hot. Her hands are numb as a stranger's. The island is its own horizon of foliage clouds. The dawn behind shades it to shapes. This boat is a rescue boat. The sun exists. She can see it. She squints against it. She is the one being rescued, now, finally.

At the far shore there is a cliff. It's too high, five feet above the waterline, but a boy flops across a ramp like it's fine. The beast's engine won't start. She plunges the kick-starter once, twice, and she can't remember what gear she's in but it's fourth and she doesn't have any traction and the bike slides sideways, and Audrey, one foot on the ramp, pulls her leg clear and lets all two hundred pounds go as the ferry pilot cries out and the beast topples into the water to lie on the bottom as if heart-attacked on its side, its headlamp shining, her bag still knotted to it.

The ferry pilot and the boy gawk.

"How much?" says Audrey.

The pilot shakes her head.

"A hundred?" says Audrey. "Five hundred thousand? What's it worth to throw my bike in the fucking river?"

The pilot turns away.

"Hey!" Audrey calls after her, but the woman's gone deaf. She read that hostility is uncouth here. Audrey drops her last 100,000 into the tangle of wet rope at the bottom of the boat. She stumps down the ramp onto the island, ignoring the boy.

The sun melts the dewdrops gold. Trees loll fiery magenta flowers into the orange-mud road, more a path than a road, really, while splendid oil-green roosters plump and caw in the doorways of yellow and turquoise houses. It's a small village. Children in their uniforms, and monks in their orange robes, and bicycles, and dogs. A white couple in white linen take their coffee on a terrace overhanging the water. The man is petite, balding, with wireframe glasses. A young white family orders their eggs *en plein air* among paper lanterns and embroidered pillows. A white woman raises her device's eye and steals a picture of a shopkeeper kneeling, dolloping rice into a monk's basket. She takes another of two girls walking with their arms around each other. She lowers the lens when Audrey invades its field, and turns instead to a wall turreted with glittering towers: a temple, with monks coming in and out, carrying their parasols. One of the turrets, as Audrey approaches, is brand new, six feet tall, bright pink, heaped with offerings. Flowers, burning incense, bananas. A glossy photograph of a little girl, maybe two years old, is framed. Three women pray under it, feeding cash into a small fire, blue and red and green. What had the consul said? That Catie had believed the girl would move out of the road. The children always do. They're so used to motorbikes. They're very canny, usually, not like kids at home, but this girl didn't, god, it was completely shocking, how it happened, it was such a tragedy.

And then, the hotel: just how she dreamed it. Dark streams of wood and ivory plaster; rough stone and polished fronds. Bamboo fans spin above empty chairs on the veranda. A glimpse of a turquoise pool.

Inside the wrought doors, a room aches with light. A white woman, papery and wrenlike, wrapped in blues, crowned in a braid of white-gold hair, comes from beneath a high arch. She presses her smiling palms together. "*Bienvenue à La Folie.*"

Audrey doesn't have money. All her life, she's only used other people's currency. But Catie's money is still good here. Catie's trust. Catie knows what she deserves. Audrey puts her empty palms together and bows.

The woman's gracious arm lifts a bell from the desk, and at its chime a silver tray bearing a crystal decanter of water floats forward, tendered cautiously and invisibly by, yes, another of the world's million million slaves.

Pre-Occupants

I thought the key prerequisite would be our psychological capacity to drink each other's filtered urine. Paul and I are high-humidity people. It's warm in here and we're both vigorous. In transit, the hygrometer warns us if our sweat and exhalations are going to damage the instrumentation. For Paul's semen, there are only two sustainable options: I swallow it or he ejaculates directly into the waste tube. Only the former is palatably human. Not just the old-earthy pornographic appeal, but the anxiety of losing still-viable parts of ourselves to the void. My body harvests enzymes, sugars, and acids; it does half the filtration work before I urinate and our machine does the rest. The crystal distillate drips into the hydro tank. We slurp from it, make coffee with it. We're in transit for six months, screwing constantly.

When we arrive, the final stagger is our landing legs snapping under us—a yardstick drop to the bedrock. We unstrap and drag ourselves to the windows to look at the other machines: white, turretless tanks, black eyes under angled shells. The omnistorm skims over everything. The air's just one rusted twilight, even with the statite refractors frying us from midpoint. The far machine is gritty as a mollusk: Tava and Will have been here four years. Muriel and Gord's machine is clearer and closer, with black print reading MUSKOX12A342. They've been here for two. A pair of pressure suits hangs off each machine like silver fingerlings sucking scum off a shark's belly. We radio our greetings over. "Welcome!" says Gord. That's it.

We're useless for days. Paul twitches at resistance bands while I lean clammily against each of the portholes, one after the other, looking out in all directions. In good light, if I brace myself and dip my knees, I can see the skyline rimming the lowest mountains, which are to the west. We can't look up. We can't see the sky, just whatever falls from it. So far: diluted sun, heavy dirt.

Paul thumbs my spine, puts his conch mouth against my ear. Even with his face carved out and his shoulders caved from transit, Paul is still as handsome as a separate species. We deflate, skin puddling, legs parted by each other's faces. Often, we pull apart to catch our breath and relax the musculature. Mid-orgasm, my foot cramps and I curl away to nurse it.

Three days, then Gord comes over to pick up the supplies we've hauled. Everything we'll build here is delivered in fragments because every freighted pound costs the Foundation two hundred and seventy thousand. Gord drives from his machine to ours in a little white transport with a jolting trailer. In his suit, he's a clown in a clown car. Roofless, flapping little doors, plastic windscreen, miniature steering wheel. It looks like an airport baggage cart. It's marked MUSKRAT23404AA6.

He shoulders out of his suit's backport, drags himself up through our floor. I don't get up from my stool. We've pulled shirts on, but our wet skin suctions to all the vinyl. "Come in," Paul says, hovering. "Good to see you."

"Welcome," says Gord again. He wipes his hands on his t-shirt, and when he shakes, his grip is fish-boned. His smiling teeth are eroded. His skull is too large for his dew-lapped neck. White sodium vees his solar plexus. He's the only person I've seen besides Paul in six months, and I have years of isolation training, but his smell is astonishing. Grease and fluids float off him into our air. He's spattering a trail like a fryer.

"Have a seat. Have some—" Paul bustles for the nutrition slurry, which is mostly amino acids, oligosaccharides, and triglycerides, plus vitamins and minerals.

"Ha, lord, no," says Gord. "Mercy." He sits down with me at the hinged aluminum plank. Two years here and he's a gnome wearing the pelt of a man. I've lost an inch of height already. Bone mass goes at one percent a month. Paul is doing better, but he had more muscle and bone to start with. Transit was worst. Now that we've arrived we won't recover, but we might brake the plunge.

"I'm kidding," says Gord, fumbling at his shoulder straps. "Nectar of the gods, right? But actually I brought you, uh, these. Anyway I remember what it was like, getting here."

He presents two plexiglass ring boxes. One strawberry in each. Pink heart fruit with a curlicue sprig.

Paul opens the lid, sniffs his fruit twice then eats it, greenery and all. I slide mine across the aluminum to look at it.

"That," Paul says. "How did—"

"Can't live on sludge forever," Gord says, and laughs. I glance at Paul. We ate the slurry exclusively for three years before we even left the ground. It satisfies the body wholly.

"Thank you," Paul says.

"It's beautiful," I say. I nudge my plastic box with my knuckle.

"Don't mention it. So. I'll pull what's marked out of your hold," Gord says. "I guess the manifest has your gadgets cordoned off and flagged."

"The launch tower. It's the most important," I tell him.

"No doubt," says Gord. "I'll set that up for you first thing."

"I think—" I say.

"May as well get started though, am I right?" Gord stands back up.

Paul opens his mouth, eyes following Gord's preparatory movements: hand on shoulder strap, shifting weight.

"I'll see you two around," says Gord. He shakes Paul's hand. He lowers himself into his suit, and for hours we can hear him scraping around like a raccoon in the guts of our machine as he loads up the muskrat. Then we watch him ferry several loads over to his own machine. And then, much later, he delivers a set of six hatboxes to Will and Tava.

I find one of his black hairs on the floor, one in the vestibule, and a handprint like a comma on the brushed grain of the airlock's hatch.

This morning we've been running on the vacuum treadmills. It is minus-forty-eight degrees Celsius outside, the wind is a steady seventy kilometres per hour. Inside, the temperature is twenty-nine and the relative humidity fifty-five. Outside, the humidity is negligible. The pressure is negligible. The carbon cycle is stopped dead. I can't see Will and Tava's machine through the dirt, but Gord is out there shovelling preliminary ditches. In sixty years we hope to raise the atmospheric pressure to Alps-like levels, which would be enough to suck a sheet of manufactured gases close to the ground. Another twenty years and breathing might be possible, with a respirator. Six years ago I paid twenty-three thousand dollars to cut out my uterus as part of the qualification process. In one hundred years the Foundation will send a breeding pair.

Paul, with shining shoulders and sweat runnelling his collarbones, comes to stand at the window with me. We only ever wear underwear now. The whole machine's wet with us. I pinch my hip's putty skin as I watch Gord stab his shovel. Pause. Lift. Again.

"Spaceman digging ditches." Paul names it like a painting. He takes my hand and I stop pinching. I lean my breast against his shoulder and tuck a thumb into his wet armpit. It's not that we smell the same but that our smells offer an identical comfort. There have been times of high stress—pre-landing, the exams, the curtains—where I took the sheet we sleep under and cupped it over my face and inhaled, repeatedly inhaled.

After Gord left our machine I ignored my strawberry. Later, Paul glanced at it, and I took it from the box and put it in his mouth. He chewed and swallowed it. I kissed him and swiped the taste of it—molecular alien, time-traveller—from his mouth, clambered up him to crawl after it. He dropped back into what used to be my pilot's chair, me fingering aside last stretches of fabric to harden his cock up and sink onto it.

Paul says, "I hope Tava has a good view of him digging."

"I don't know how they're going to record us," I say.

"They can probably imagine it."

"Then why not just stay home."

"Us in the cockpit's not so exciting."

"What else would she paint? The rock."

"Omnistorm number seventy-three."

"Omnistorm number seventeen thousand one hundred and eighty."

Since I landed us we've repurposed the sensors and torn out the obsoletes. A trash pile of vinyl shock cushions, knotty wiring, and aluminum facing has accumulated under the dumbwaiter airlock. Gord magpies all this off for use elsewhere, without knocking. Gord also assembled my launch tower, as promised, aligned my hundreds of tiny virile rockets into ready patterns. Strapped in our chairs, paralysis settles. The monitor is a yoke. Drifts of follicles and our scratched epidermis sludge the gaps between keys. Our oils blur the aluminum in favoured places.

We count shifts in quarter cycles. Sleep, work, break, work, repeat. We celebrate the day's extra forty minutes at noon, usually by screwing. Sometimes Paul reads. Until we die we'll be catching comets. I am responsible for exo-monitoring, launching outbound rockets to snare the passing icebergs. Paul guides them in, dragging them off-course towards our southern pole. They gush frozen water and ammonia while the blast melts the icecaps. His reports focus on average mean temperature, sulfur hexafluoride buildup. In a hundred years we'll have denuded the solar system of all eight thousand, and both poles will be wholly melted, leaving the surface twenty-five percent drinkable water. We average three asteroids a day, with a wide variance from seventeen to none for weeks. They come as they will. The Foundation denies the mathematical possibility that I could snare one too large and bury us all a kilometre deep in shrapnel.

We also nurse a bacteria swarm, seventy thousand species of lichen and algae. These are located in one square metre of transparent plexiglass shelving near the waste tube. The moulds alone: mustard, butter, mint, forest, turquoise, teal, lavender, violet, carmine, rust, corpse grey, cloud blue. I pull them out, tray by tray, every square centimetre sealed and glowingly alive, except for the blackboxed ones tucked away from the light.

I don't have a nail file and my fingers are flaking in sedimentary layers as I use one to clean the other. They get to ugly angles from the way I peel them off. The occasional hangnail.

"Put in a request," he says.

"Waste twenty grams on a nail file."

"Maybe Muriel has one."

"I don't want it."

"Muriel's?" he says.

"Anything," I say. "I'm not asking."

Nothing from Will and Tava. I really thought there would be more chatter on the radio. It's the isolation training: the cure is also the cause.

During one calm sunrise, Gord heads west across the triangle. But it isn't Gord, because there are two suits dangling from Gord and Muriel's machine and only one at Will and Tava's. So is it Will? He climbs into the muskrat and drives out of my porthole's frame. I haul myself to the northernmost hole, but he's on his way past an outcrop, hunched against occasional gusts, driving into the flats.

Later, Gord is out digging a new ditch, a fourth—it's just a year until the next pair lands and makes us a parallelogram, brings silky connector tubes that will line our sightlines and allow us all to crawl around tapping on each other's airlocks—and he doesn't look overly alarmed that the muskrat is gone.

"That was Tava that drove off," Paul says when I go and stand over the cockpit. "Definitely a woman."

"You can't tell."

"I can tell between Muriel and Gord," he says.

"Because of her tool belt."

"I was looking out the scope. It was Tava." Paul's voice, when he's irritated, indicates I should shut up.

I shut up. I'm developing a rough patch of skin on my left tricep. I rub it and the skin whitens and drifts away, leaving small yellow-and-red bumps of varying size.

I pry one of the suit-ports open in the vestibule and look down into the well of cold I've unstoppered. I paddle my hand in the temperature gradient. I tell the suit to test and prepare itself while I go back to the living room and put on all my layers of clothing, which still stink with the anxiety of blast-off. Putting on socks is a small strangulation. The leggings are stranger. They sag. When I return, the suit's pressure is satisfactory and the thermocline's equalized. I dip my swabbed appendages into it. Feet slide into feet, hands into hands.

"Are you leaving?"

I twist, catch him in the corner of my eye. He is framed in the halo of my backport, its bullseye is my nape. Once, he left me to clean myself up after our orgasms, then came back and found me masturbating.

I modulate my voice, "Not far."

He hulks over me. It's unpleasant to keep twisting, and I can't see him, so I settle forward into my dangle. "Would you like to come?" I ask. Through the suit's visor I can see the soil and rock in nanoscale granularity, sweeping itself clean. My boots hang thirty centimetres above. I swing my feet in them.

"Don't be an idiot," Paul says, and slaps the lever back to seal me out.

All I can smell is myself. The suit checks and confirms my independence. I grip the grab bars and lower to the surface. Beside me, the other suit hangs from the neck like a kitten or a convict.

I turn to look up at the closed port. Of course he cannot come. One of us has to let the other back in.

I step out from under our machine's belly into the omnistorm. It's like midnight in the North Atlantic. I might as well be clinging to an orange foam vest. The wind churns like I'm pulling from the propeller's maelstrom. At any second the blade that powers this place might cleave me, or a whipping, thousand-ton anchor chain might snap and seize me. The half-formed atmosphere is shrieking about the carnage happening in the other hemisphere: twenty billion megaton collisions digging cradles two kilometres deep for the unborn oceans. If I ended my bombardment today, this storm still wouldn't settle for a decade.

Gord has gone inside. All the suits are hanging in place. I examine Gord's ditches. Two metres down into the regolith, one across. One hundred metres between each machine, including the smoothed-out foundation for the approaching pair. The trenches are sealed with long tongues of rock-bolted tarpaulin that flap loose in the places where the wind is shovelling dirt back in.

I walk into our field of light turbines. The cone-faced flowers are child-height. Today the storm is so dark they don't know where to look. They turn to shake their heads at each other. I touch the crowns of their gritty craniums. Then for a second the wind dies and the light's filter unhinges to let the sun slosh down clear. All of us look up.

"Testing, testing," says the radio during third shift.

Paul and I look at each other. He moves first.

"I'm not sure exactly what—" He pokes his face at the mic. "Hello?"

"Hello. Paul?"

"Yes?"

"It's Tava. How are you? Listen, we saw your wife out on her promenade and Will realized he hasn't even interviewed the both of you yet!"

Paul stares at me. After a bit, his mouth moves: "Oh. Oh, no. I guess... he hasn't."

"We thought you might drop by for dinner if you're free this week."

"Oh," Paul says, "Dinner?"

"We'd love to have you."

He doesn't take his eyes off me. One of my hands keeps flipping onto its back in the air.

"Yeah sure," Paul says. "That sounds great."

"Does any day in particular work for you?"

"Well, any time, really."

I tap the monitor in front of me with the backs of my fingernails.

"Oh," he says. "Except we're babysitting the comets. So actually now that I think about it. One of us has to be here."

"Oh, I see."

There's some murmuring. Paul scowls at me.

Tava again: "That's really too bad. Those routines aren't something you could transfer over here to our machine I guess."

"Well, maybe," Paul says, because he is amenable.

I am shaking my head. We are ultra-specialized, compared to the other machines, which are built only to keep bodies alive and have half our brainpower. I don't say this out loud to the radio. I could be in another segment of the machine, oblivious to this conflict. Sweat runs down my ribcage.

"Actually," Paul says. "My wife's saying no, we can't. Our setup here is… complicated."

"Oh, that's too bad," says Tava. "What bad news."

I tuck my chin down and jab random functions on my monitor.

"But listen," Paul says. "You're welcome to come over here instead. We'd love to have you."

"No, no, we couldn't just invite ourselves over."

"No, no," says Paul. "We'd really love it. Like you say, we haven't even met yet."

I look back up, mouth open. If he'd look at me I'd flip my hand again.

"Well, in that case we'll bring dinner."

"Don't be ridiculous," says Paul again. "We're cooking."

"A salad, at least," says the radio.

Paul laughs as he shakes his head and hangs up. He comes to sit back down, smiling.

"They have vegetables?" I ask.

"Weren't they joking?" he says.

I don't answer. I don't know. We've been here fourteen months.

His hair is getting shaggy. "We should do haircuts," I tell him. I never look at mine because the first time he cut it I was angry. We're better without mirrors. We look to each other. From the feel of it the patch at the top of my spine is growing out faster than the rest, as always. When I look at my reflection in the porthole my eyes are so deep in my skull I can't see them, just the lights of the other machines: one tri-eyed, one cyclopsed.

Paul digs out the clippers. They're supposed to suck away the detritus through the waste tube, but there's dandruff and slick shafts like black paper cuts on his shoulders and closed eyes. Everything sticks or floats. I pet his curls forward into a charming cowlick, grade the sides precisely. When he shears me, everything is bald even. He has never discerned the difference between "buzz" and "pixie." I have always had two concerns about this: visibility of pimples, like the current triad on my neck, and how, as a child, I had large ears.

After he's shaved me, we screw. As soon as I come, he pulls away and pulses his cock into the waste tube, fisting into its mouth. Our machine's apparatus is a pearly transparent worm drifting around his legs as it sucks. His spine curls fetally. After he disengages, he hands me a cloth to wipe myself.

Tava and Will put a steaming chicken pot pie in the airlock. I pull it out of its silver case as Paul helps them dock.

Tava pulls herself up into our machine with overlong arms. She is shrunk-faced. She wears bangs and eyeliner and a black dress that's tight enough to show the narrow rolls at her waist and also how her breasts are mildly lopsided in that they are unrestrained and glance in googly directions. She has an authoritative mouth, but with her snub nose she looks just a little bit doggish. Her paintings are mostly of cities. On Earth I read an article that said her treatment of city as landscape, her lack of distinction between human and natural, is why she was chosen. The article called her derivative and sentimental. Another article I read said she once painted covers for science-fiction novels—green, many-limbed animals—implying also that she was a poor choice, if not the worst choice. One of her paintings, which looked to me like a cliff and sunbathers, sold for eighty million dollars after she and Will were named to document the settlement. Tava was the first human on Mars. Will was a close second.

Will is egg-headed and his arms are also too long, and tattooed. Paul read his book on the way here. He is fifteen years older than she is. Their age gap was a concern: it increases the likelihood one of them will die and one of them will be left alone to burn in their machine while the rest of us are helpless to suffocate the grief. But the Foundation's physicians did their Death Index assessments. Now we all swallow a micro-regimen of tetrodotoxins to even things out.

"Where did you get this?" I say, cradling the blue-flowered Corning Ware.

"It's a family recipe," says Tava. "I hope you like it. Oh god, you both eat meat, don't you? I didn't even think to ask."

191

My body has not digested solids in quantities greater than seventy grams—three squares of chocolate on my last birthday on Earth—in fifty-eight months.

Will presents a litre of water in a clear glass bottle with a rubberized seal. "Our own private distillation," he says, and Tava laughs and pincers his waistline with both hands.

"God I miss wine," she says. "They didn't send you up with any, I bet."

"Unfortunately," says Paul.

"Us either," Will says. "But we swap waters with the Bateses over there, just to get something new on the palate."

"Do you mind if I use your washroom?" She waggles her fingers. Her nails are glossed and even.

"Please," I say, and lead her to the nook where the waste tube coils. I pull the plastic divider around for her privacy. I gaze into my dormant lichens. The prismatic light farm looks festive. A Christmas cube. I miss my fat, anxious mother.

"Those two," Tava says through the plastic. "Not to gossip, but I have never seen a mother and son get along so well."

"We've never met Muriel," I say. I take two steps away.

"Us either!" says Tava, and I pause. There's a small sound that I try not to hear. A motor whirrs. Then the suction hose slurps. Tava sighs.

"I see her out maintaining the light turbines," I say.

"Her and that magenta tool belt. It's the only thing that colour on the whole planet. Has it ever occurred to you that it's just Gord out there? Wearing the tool belt?"

"No," I say.

"She had him when she was fourteen. That's why they're so close," Tava says. She brushes the privacy curtain aside. "Will reads all the files, it's his process. He's honestly so excited to interview you two."

My file says Bachelor of Applied Arts in Business Admin. I spent sixteen years in Titusville, twelve in Tampa, seven in training. My target death range is 52-53; ninety-six percent probability of organ failure (environmental conditions).

Will has produced long-stemmed glasses out of the insulated case. They ting when jostled.

He pours four from his own bottle. The liquid is carbonated. How do they carbonate it? "It's great to finally meet you two. How goes the bombardment?"

"Ongoing," I say.

We don't have plates. Will produces plates out of the insulated case. We don't have cutlery. Will produces cutlery.

"You said you'd bring a salad," I say.

"Did we? Oh no," Will looks to Tava.

"You're disappointed," she says.

"No, I'm not. I didn't mean." They stare at me. I'm miserable. "I was curious."

Paul stares at the empty plate in his hands.

"Tava was craving something warm and filling, so we thought."

"We…" I say. "Don't we…?" I try again.

"It's November," says Tava.

Paul jumps in: "It smells delicious. We haven't had anything like this in ages."

"Why thank you, Paul!" Tava smiles at him.

"We were just saying on the way over we think it's a pity that we never see the comets," says Will, spooning steaming heaps of flake pastry and meat. Gravy.

"Oh I know," says Tava. "The collisions must be spectacular. How can we see them?"

I look at Paul.

"That's not really—" he says.

"You can't go over there," I say.

"Obviously driving would take months." Will agrees, "We'd die."

"But you could aim one closer couldn't you," says Tava. "So we could see it."

"God, no," says Paul.

"You think we'd die?" says Will.

"I haven't even seen one in the sky, is the problem," says Tava. "Easily the most visually crucial act we'll commit in this place."

"And the most important to settlement," says Will.

"It's basically the same as an H-bomb. Clouds," Paul says.

"And then," Tava adds, "the *crater*."

I am worried about the added carbonation from the fizzing water we're all holding—taken from their system and released into ours—even though it is negligible, millilitres. The cycle is closed. They are also adding a litre of water to us. We must make them drink a litre of ours. Their water tastes briskly green. It's neutral, acidless. A bit of sodium, some sweet linger at the end. The carbonation is especially alien. I anticipate heartburn. Why are they carbonating their water? Where did they grow chicken?

"The other thing we want to do," says Tava.

"Our other big plan—I know, we have so many—have you seen the map regarding the other settlement?"

"Of course they've seen it."

"Right, so if we could bring back one of those machines. Or a few. I mean, it could be ongoing."

"They're, what would you say, two hundred clicks out?"

"Basically just sitting there."

"The space would be so useful, we're thinking. Like a little community centre. We could put in a garden. I guess you guys don't have…" Tava peers around as if to check that we do not, indeed, have a garden.

"What other settlement?" I say.

"The bandwidth crew," Tava says. She looks from Paul to me. "For the data-stream infrastructure. First priority."

"I thought you were the first," I say to her.

Everyone laughs, even Paul. I look at him.

"We've been out there. It's not so far. Seven hours return."

"But what about the people?" I say.

"The people?" Tava glances at Will, who shrugs.

"Almost all recycled by now," he says.

When they leave, I find blonde hair clumped in the clippers' fanged mouth. She shaved a part of herself using our blade. The strands are short, near translucent. She is out there, wearing one painless, hairless stripe.

At noon the next day, Paul dresses. His leggings float around his calves. He puts Tava's clean casserole dish into the dumbwaiter airlock, glass lid upside down. He lowers into his suit. I stand over him. His face has weathered down to ridges. I want to tell him how horrible it is out there. I want to trim his urge from him like a fingernail. But he is closed to complaint. "Shut up," he says. His body, which I love, is already strung outside in the storm. I can't go with him. I slap the lever back and our machine locks against him. One of us has to let the other back in. What closeness is there? Is there such a thing as being adequately close?

Retirement

In the morning my molars are welded together. I palm around for clothes, hook and drag them back into the sweat-wet tunnel of my sleeping bag. I brought a girl here in the black last night: a twenty-minute blind pilgrimage made by barefoot feel and the arterial knowledge that this valley has been mine from birth. She wasn't from here. If she even knew where I'd led her it would've taken her a sober daylit hour to walk back down into town. My tent is hidden in the trees at the top of the cliff that I used to stand on when I was a kid and thought I might be close to killing myself. If she walked straight out of its mouth she would've gone right over. I unzip the door, crawl into the cold dew. Roughage churns in the river below. I have a tourist's perfect view of the valley's flatbed. The engine bridge is a black lattice-work trap. Past it, Main Street's arrowed right at me so I can count the cars. Beyond it: low-rise condos, big-box stores, chain hotels, and the highway slipstream seaming the valley. Then up, across, at eye level, there's the empty oil-money mansions, still shadowed while the sun rolls out behind them, veins of their new laneways rotting up the slopes of the mountains' south faces. To the right, the valley yawns into foothills. To the left, it narrows and climbs. I'm sure she made it fine. When I was a kid I'd stand here and wonder if I'd take the three steps. I'd watch the big alpine ravens croak around and hope for their pity. One morning the assistant coach said, in front of everyone, "Evan, was that you standing up on the cliffs looking so sad last night?" So I stopped coming up here. Intellectually, I understand that some people just don't feel pain like this. Their neurons never learned it. Why bother telling you what the town looks like when every time I look up the weather has transformed the mountains into something new? This morning the peaks have white auras like angels. They've sucked the sky clear. My home is a place so beautiful it will burn you alive just to look at it.

On the far side of the quarry, my sister commands a battalion of recumbent drunks. The water is a pit of black icemelt with two newly manufactured beaches and thirty-foot rock faces from which teenagers hurl themselves. This far up their flanks, the peaks bend over us. On the near beach, a few lean children splash. My sister's friends are girls on towels in flowered bikinis and wide sunglasses with bottles in their hands. Their bellies pooch but their legs are long and hairlessly tan. The guys wear tropical-hued tank tops and knock-off Ray-Bans. They work at hotels, restaurants, sports-equipment stores, or, if they've made something of themselves since they graduated high school, auto-body shops and real-estate offices. Close up, they are grouped in legible clutches. I count at least six who actively don't speak to me. Everyone is well-supplied with coolers and towels and bulging bags even though at any moment the mountains will cock their heads between us and the sun and everyone will get instantly chilly.

My sister Alex has a laser-cut laugh. She's wearing a neon bra and a scrap of shirt that sticks to her breasts and ribs. My beer cans roll over in their box. An honour guard of girls glare at me like SPCA cats as I approach. I haven't socialized with these people in two years. It's been six since high school. There are three girls here that I've slept with, a population that combines one hundred percent with the six—there were instances of public overlap, unfortunately—who don't speak to me.

"The golf course called Silas in," Alex says of her missing boyfriend. A girl—Nicki Rosso—jerks up and takes her towel with her as I settle down in the sand. Alex has a bottle of grapefruit Perrier, which she's drinking over ice in a gold-rimmed tumbler I recognize from my father's dusty collection. The 1988 Winter Olympics logo is also gold. You could buy them—tumblers, wine glasses, flutes, etc.—at the gas station. I was four. My fat hands clutched the eternal flame while my mother held me in her arms.

"Why?" I say. "Some oil baron shit himself on the green?"

"Weddings," she shrugs. Alex is so scrawny her shoulders poke through her skin. Her thinness masquerades as morphology. She and her mom moved in with my dad and me the summer I started high school. She was three years younger. We spent every after-school alone together and she never spoke and she never ate. My eating was equally controlled, but my intake was massive and precise. I had to rebuild my wracked body every three hours to stave off shakes, despair, collapse. My coaches would send home the weekly meal plan and Suze, Alex's mom, would say "Can't we swap you for something useful, like a polo pony?" I was in training six hours a day, or else I was gone racing in Scandinavia, or where the fuck ever.

Alex is seven months pregnant and her belly weighs as much as she does. "Shotgun?" I say, cracking a can. I can't even look at it.

"Shut up," Alex says. "If they keep him all night I'll be so pissed. What is that, organic beer?"

"Yes," I say. "I'm taking care of myself these days."

I can hear the talk behind me coming from Nicki and the other girls: "Does he actually think this is ok?"

Alex cocks her head, her mouth quirked. She raises an eyebrow at me. Her legs spindle into the sand, feet sunk up to the knobs of her anklebones. She's marble, some immaculate relic. Except the belly. I reach out and flick it hard with a fingernail.

"Fuck! Evan!"

I drain half my can. "So are you two gonna get married or what."

"What? No, god." she says.

"He's been living with you for like a year," I say.

"Yeah, believe me, I've been counting the days."

"I'm going to go. I can't stay here," one of the girls says.

"Nicki, christ. He should be the one that leaves," says another.

"He pisses in the shower. I'd say don't tell him I told you that but honestly I think he likes being so disgusting." Alex sounds legitimately fond.

I grimace. "So names you're thinking, what, Bobby Joe? BJ, Bertha. Charlene...?"

"This is bullshit. I'm not sitting here like this," another girl says.

Alex snorts. "Speaking of trash, you live in a tent, Evan. At least his parents are lawyers."

"Explains his personality," I say.

"Look, buddy. You gotta go."

I crane my neck. Luke Chenier is wearing a bored expression on his thuggy narc face. Behind him, Nicki is looking away, teary. Other girls—Marie, Emily, Samantha, Sandra, Jessica—glare back.

"What the fuck, Luke," says Alex. "He's my brother."

"Oh hey, Nicki. Didn't see you there," I say.

"You gotta go," Luke says again. His hands are spread, firm. He's maybe the only guy here from my year. Started bartending at The Drake at eighteen and never quit. In high school he played running back for the Wolverines and dated Alex for at least a year. I heard them screwing through the air vents. She told me he cried when she dumped him.

"Why is everyone being so fucking dramatic?" says Alex. "What are you, in grade nine? Nicki, christ. Get over it."

I stand up and realize it's a mistake, it looks like a concession. "Nicki," I say, trying to catch her eye. "How've you been? You look great."

Nicki does not look great. She looks a little swollen, a little pink. It's hard to say exactly why she's acting so shattered. I would've guessed Samantha hated me more. I would've guessed they'd hate each other, but Sam's hand is on Nicki's shoulder.

"You're the worst thing that has ever happened to me," says Marie. I lift a hand. I always forget about Marie.

"Die in a fucking fire," says Nicki.

I swig from my beer can. The furies glare. I will not leave. I take off my shirt—fucked if my body isn't the best they ever laid hands on—and stroll to the waterline. "Thanks for being real, girls," I call. Alex laughs.

The peaks are neon pink and loom like tombstones, closer than anything, closer than the glimmering water in the middle of this well. The far beach is blue and deserted. Knee-deep, hip-deep, feeling forward along the serrated rock. The water shrivels my balls. I take another step and fall off the edge.

This was a mining town. This was a quarry. At the bottom of this hole there are machines abandoned in the black. I drop, kicking over the emptiness. Eyes open, the murk grades azure down to the void. Whoever's down there, they asked for it.

I get emails from Claire, sometimes. They say things like, *I just beat the shit out of this hotel treadmill* and *Lydia is snoring I miss you* and *Call me* and *Do me a favour and confirm you're alive please*. She sends pictures of fogged churches on virgin routes, light beers in dark-wood pubs, a tree with a unicorn carved into the bark. They've replaced me with a nineteen-year-old from Sherbrooke with cystic acne. I wake up in my tent on the cliff thinking about Alex rubbing against me through our respective jeans, under a blanket on the couch while our parents drank next door. We kissed through the backs of our hands, palms pressed between our mouths, so it wouldn't be real.

I stop by the house to charge up my phone. I grew up here, a trailer in a trailer park with pink glitter stucco, red-brown trim. My dad built a long, sloppy, lengthwise deck. He grills every night. There's a firepit in the yard where I used to host parties for my friends. Alex and Silas still do. There's a basement crawlspace that's jammed exclusively with my old skis, goggles, helmets, poles, medals. My mom would've sold the detritus as soon as I outgrew it; she never let anything but the medals and ribbons accumulate. But Suze smokes indoors and you can't even open the door to her sewing room—which was once my bedroom—because of eBay.

I plug in my phone and go through the cupboards looking for something edible. Bran flakes. I haven't trained in the month I've been here, but the only difference between my body now and my body two years ago is that my knees hurt. Okay, and last week when I hiked up Grotto Canyon my posture was crumpled, and I didn't feel like bounding around off boulders. Even my sweat was pathetic, drippy. But what am I going to do, buy a gym membership? I shovel fiber mush into my mouth and look at the gold medal where it hangs over the fireplace. Two and a half years ago I burned up the fifteen kilometre classic in thirty-seven minutes and dark-horsed the Swedish favourite. His breath hollowed out in my ears, his ski tips clattered my heels on the curves. A coarse, constant chop. The sound of the crowd at the finish line swamped the world. Out of the trees, down the run. The whites of my periphery clear. I didn't look back until they'd draped me in triumph, ten metres past the line. The Swede was rounding the bend. Barely leading the Austrians. Sixteen seconds. I don't know what happened. I was not supposed to win.

Silas comes out of the back bedroom in saggy black underwear and the bloom of his own unwash. He's lanky with a farmer's tan, dumb as rocks.

"Good. They didn't find you and kill you in your sleep," he says, rubbing crust out of his doe eyes.

"Alex still in bed?"

"Her shift started at six."

"Shit," I say. "Is there coffee?"

He shuffles to the kitchen and shifts cautious tectonics in the sink while I arrange myself on the dented sofa and look at the same vaulted ridge of peaks that has backgrounded every glance down this street since infancy. They glint at me.

"What are you doing today? We should blow up the raft and bring it down to the engine bridge."

"Work, man," Silas doesn't look at me. "Majorly understaffed. I haven't had a day off since April."

"Huh," I say.

"Offer's still open, obviously."

"Carrying rich guys' balls? I wish. I don't think I have it in me."

"To get a job?" Silas says.

For a second I want to shove him, and then I want to walk out the door, casual, but then the coffee machine beeps. As he hands me a mug I say, "So how long till you guys move out again?"

"Move out?"

"Oh wait, you're actually gonna raise it here?"

His hair dangles over his beak as he transports sugar into his mug. "That's the plan. You know what rent is like." He glances at me. The *or maybe you don't* is silent.

"I guess that means Suze is clearing her hoarder stash out of my bedroom finally."

He pulls milk out of the overpopulated fridge and waggles it. "Yeah. Nightmare. Actually. You know what would be a huge help? If you could get your stuff out of the crawlspace."

"My what?" I say.

"Your skis and shit, you know."

"Oh, that. Like, all my medals and trophies. Yeah, for sure." My voice ratchets. "No problem." I point my chin at the gold over the fireplace. "What about that one? That one okay?"

"Whatever you think is best, man." He pours milk into my cup as I hold it. He's a head taller than me. He's always seemed older than me. Capable of changing tires, splitting wood. For a second I'm childlike, not childish. He smiles at me. "That's a big load off."

I drink my coffee on the porch steps and imagine killing myself. I'd walk back to my tent, pack it up, and then step off the cliff. The satisfying part is the shock of it, everyone gaping over all my wasted potential. David Foster Wallace. John Kennedy Toole. Young Werther. The unsatisfying part is imagining Nicki and Sam and Marie and Suze and Silas and whichever asshole's banging Claire now, imagining how relieved they'd all be. Overjoyed.

Instead, I decide to go buy a few beers and a power bar and hike up Grotto again.

It was easy after Turin. The media loved me and Claire. The media loved my dead mom. Claire puts out energy like a white sun, newborn. No one doubts her smile. She spends three weeks every year training little girls to wipe out without crying. She looks like loss would slide off her. Loss would evaporate from her skin and sparkle in the air around her. She'll be great on the speaking circuit. I've never seen her read anything besides comedian memoirs. I didn't win anything again. I was back at the top of mid-pack. I never had an exit strategy. I had nowhere else to go besides here. When I booked a ticket home in the middle of Val di Fiemme a month ago, Claire shoved my half-packed duffel off the bed and snarled, "What the fuck was the point, then?"

The trail up Grotto starts wide and gravelled, graciously coasting alongside the creek. A red-and-black runner dashes me like a deer. Then a woman pushing a muddy yellow hiking stroller. The child behind the plastic windshield is bloated pink, face streaming with liquids. It kreels toothlessly past me, conveyed helpless as an oracle harvested from its cave. I may as well be carrying a parasol. My beers are too heavy for their shitty plastic bag.

There'd always been a lot of parties. International organizations hosted galas. The ones the sponsors threw were better. Claire and the girls would appear in the hotel lobby in black dresses that draped clavicles and taut trapezius lines. Lipstick and earrings transfigured them from grim projectiles furled up in the starting blocks. Still, compared to the other guests, all of us were the same unmistakable animal: ludicrous with goggle tans, windburned raw. We'd smile and talk to women too elegant for muscle, men who'd jiggle if they fucked. Even people our age: a skinny guy carrying a platter of stemware would hack a smoker's lungful into his elbow. What would the girl behind the bar look like naked? A nice girl who drank to get drunk, who thought of food in terms of likes and dislikes, who had time to go to college. We circulated, said our bromides, smiled. White-clothed tables were spread with what amounted to installation pieces. One glass of wine. Two max. We were not expected to be thoughtful. Rich men giggled when I bummed a smoke on the balcony. They looked over my shoulder for the coaches. "Very glamorous," one drawled approvingly. "Do I make you want to buy something?" I asked. "Down jacket? Travel insurance?" They made me wear my gold medal around my neck, over my tuxedo. Everyone kept giggling. The nicotine made me nauseous. The taste of the cigarette in my mouth was like my mother. They were *supposed* to envy me.

When I came home the whole town was decked out for me. Penny Archambault, the big realtor, gave me a car that read in giant blue script CONGRATULATIONS EVAN HARMS OLYMPIC GOLD MEDALIST TURIN 2006!

I made out with a lot of girls in that car, using psychological tricks I'd picked up from Orin Incandenza. Claire was in
Peru. She'd assumed I'd go with her. I took too long to tell
her I didn't care about Machu Picchu and so that whole period
was radio silence between us. We'd been together since we
were what, seventeen? If she wasn't sleeping around down
there I don't know what she was doing. All I had to do was
look anguished and tell a girl about how desperately, eternally
in love with Claire I was and simultaneously how terrifying
it was to be so overwhelmed by this new girl's eyes, mouth,
kindness, beauty etc., and I'd get comforted and blown and
the girl—a Québécoise or Australian working the ski hills, an
American tourist, someone's cousin from the UK, Samantha,
Marie, Nicki—would go home silent and superior, post-dra-
matic, tasked with the sacred charge of keeping our secret.

The air in the canyon is dry with juniper and birdwhis-
tle. Rocks break through the packed dirt of the path like
spined mammals surfacing. The creek gushes clear over
pink-flecked, black-glossed boulders, pooling neck-deep then
roiling onward. Sticks gather in eddies, but no moss or algae.
Everything is holy and clean. The canyon closes overhead,
cool as a crypt beneath the peak's basilica. Wagner. Byron.
Kant. The sublime is fractal: start with the quartz sparkle in
wet stone and zoom out to the bitter cliffs shadowed in a sliver
of sun, zoom out to the ruined peak whose gash you're clambering up, zoom out to the vertebral range, then the valley's
mandible: a hundred billion beauties, none of them attainable
though they are valueless, free, ubiquitous. The only thing this
place exports, besides athletes, is wedding photographers and
watercolourists. Tourists come here to gawk, and we abjure
them, but we can't comprehend this place either. Gaping out
the window as your vehicle speeds past on the highway isn't

improved by doing it twenty times a day for two decades because, either way, one day you'll see the familiar, stony visages on a screen in an airport and they will be man-made, glassy, with a bank's monogram in the corner. All you can ever do is wrap the world in a circle around yourself, and look at it.

Two hundred metres ahead, where the canyon jags right, rocks engulf the woman and her yellow stroller. Newborn boulders grind themselves down to teeth as they churn over each other. The noise is delayed, amplified, repeated. I hear it in stutters. I sprint. As I sprint I'm afraid that the rock-slide is going to fill the canyon, yet I am sprinting towards it. The boulders remap the creek in a fog of dust and spray. The yellow stroller is upside down in there, wheels mangled. The churn rolls over itself. The stroller drops. Drops again. I fear the baby is dead. I can't see the woman. I clamber across the living rift. The water is icemelt, the rocks hack my shins. They are the size of vehicles, of household appliances. They've stopped, and as I step onto them they move again. The baby is shrieking. The stroller rests, half-submerged in icy water, plastic windshield intact. The baby is slung from its straps, blotched red but unbloody, fat arms kicking and splashing. How did the stroller float so leafily along over the crush? I'm afraid the baby is hurt in a way that I'll hurt it worse. I have to move it. I unhook it. I hold its hot, sopping weight. I strain to see the woman. "Is he okay?" shouts a man. "There's a woman in there," I say. The wailing grates. The runner speaks into her phone. I look up the slide's chute: a raw white wound traces up and up. I cannot follow it.

At the hospital I am blanketed, cosseted, plied with liquids, acutely monitored. They murmur to me, touch me broadly like I'm high strung, a thoroughbred. I can accept this; this is a support team. They need me. In fact, they'd be just as happy if I misbehaved a little, let them fluster to calm me.

I don't shy from the reporter. I break down the most relevant minutes for him. Translate from blur to language, string a line so that time runs linearly. It's part of the job. Or it was. In Turin someone asked me, "Is there anything left you'd like to achieve in life?"

"They're not sure yet," the reporter says of the mother. "She was conscious when they pulled her out, though."

I wish I'd been the one who rescued them both. But it was the runner who pulled her out, started excavating while the emergency team was en route. A woman dropped her hiking poles to take the shrieking baby from me as soon as I came out of the rocks, bleeding. They told me a boulder toppled while I was coming back across and I jumped ten feet, easy, the baby in my arms. This is why my ankle is swollen. I don't remember anything except how the yellow stroller kept jolting downwards in the shifting rocks, like a Ferris-wheel basket.

In the paper on Thursday I am quoted as saying, "Yeah, I guess I do feel like a hero a little bit."

"I didn't say that," I tell Alex, pointing at it.

"What a fucker," says Alex.

"Don't worry about it," says Suze.

"You should sue them for libel," says Silas.

"Oh, jeez," says Suze. She is a lean little woman, wolf-ish from years smiling at customers in the grocery store.

Everyone goes to work. I lie on the couch until I can't stand the nicotine stench anymore. There are no photos of my mother in the house, except in photo albums I don't look at. Her holding me, me holding the torch.

I hobble over to The Drake for a drink. I walk because Penny Archambault didn't want to keep making lease payments after the first year, and I couldn't afford them. Luke Chenier raises his eyebrows at me because he's still taking chairs down from tables. I take a pint and a medicinal shot of Jameson without comment and find a bench on the sunny, sticky patio. My phone is a pocket watch: I haven't heard from Claire in a week. She'll call when she finds out. I could've died. People keep saying that, "You could've *died*."

By three o'clock there are people who want to talk to me. One of them is a girl with very long hair and crystals tattooed on her thighs. Her friend has breasts and is prettier. They're only here for the summer, or the weekend.

I go to get another pint and whisky, my fourth round maybe, and Luke says, "Here you go," which is more than he's said to me all afternoon.

"I saved a fucking *baby*, man," I tell him, because it's all I've been saying to anyone.

"Oh yeah. That was a good picture of you in the paper," he agrees. It was the same shot they'd used when I won gold: goggles around my neck, hair sweated wild, arms raised. The other, bigger picture: devastation. A grave mound, empty.

"That worth a drink on the house?" I lean into the bar. "Front page?"

He gazes at me, inscrutable and sober, and I raise my hands as if joking. "You think I'm such an asshole."

"No man, I don't judge." His eyes flick past me. He wipes a palm on the towel over his shoulder.

"You took Nicki and them's side at the quarry," I say.

He pretends he didn't hear me. He's serving another customer. It's the girl with the thigh tattoos. I reach down and brush one with my fingers.

She looks at me, surprised. She smiles.

"This guy's an asshole," I murmur into her ear. "Have you been up to the cliffs yet? There's this spot I love. You should see it."

She puts a bill on the bar, smiles, tucks her hair behind her ear. "I'll go ask Lisa."

"Why?" I say. Then, "I can't stop looking at you."

"Maria," says Luke. Apparently this is the girl's name. He shakes his head.

The girl looks at me, confused.

"This guy hates me," I say, too loudly. People glance over.

"Evan, you can eat a burger and sober up, or you can move it along," Luke has that bored look on his face again.

"I can't eat a fucking burger," I say. "Look at me. I haven't eaten a burger in my fucking life."

"All right, buddy," says Luke. I am suddenly afraid he'll come around the bar. I look over my shoulder for the bouncer.

"I'm going," I say. "You coming?"

The girl looks away.

I raise my hands. I retreat, limping. Listing.

Outside, I piss in the pharmacy parking lot and call Alex.

"I'm at work," she says.

"I need you," I say.

"What's wrong?"

"It's my ankle," I say. "I'm outside the pharmacy."

She pulls up in her dirty red hatchback. I'm sitting pretty straight on the bench. She's wearing a white polo shirt from the hotel, and polyester trousers. The shirt is extra large to accommodate her distended belly.

"See? Even that looks hot on you," I say.

"What's wrong with your ankle?"

"It's fucked," I say.

"What did you do? Do you need to go back to the hospital?"

"I was never gonna win shit again anyway." My tongue is thick. I speak slowly.

"Christ," she says.

"You're the only one who ever loved me," I say. I look up at her. Her mouth is wrinkled. "Why did you let him get you pregnant?"

"It's six o'clock, how are you this drunk?"

"Everyone fucking hates me." My face is wet. I wipe my nose.

"Oh yeah?" she says.

"She just let me leave," I say. "Then she kept on going like nothing even changed."

"Get in the car," she says.

I stand up, but let my ankle give out. I stumble down the curb. I'm on my hands and knees. "Why are you having that fucking baby? Do you even care about me? Why don't you want me?"

She says, "Get up, Evan."

"You're the same as me, that's why." I roll onto my back. Gravel digs into my spine. It's not enough to just look at the mountains. They have to kill you. You have to die here. My eyes are shut against the sun's glare. "Worthless."

My mother, looking at me as I looked into that mute eternal flame, her beautiful face, alive with love.

The Roar

When Dino gets back with the guests it's dark and the helicopter's chop has both dogs crying at the door. Loyola stands up from the table to pull bottles from the fridge. The girl on the couch opens her eyes.

"You can go to bed," Loyola offers.

The girl, hair greased around her face, stays put. Dino brought her home last night.

Loyola follows the dogs out the side door. They fear the rotors about the same as they fear the vacuum: they hackle and moan at the asphalt's edge while the hired hands dart under the blades. Stein unropes a pair of chamois from the game cage. Heads loll and long black devil horns scrape the paint's gloss. He carries each in his arms into the hangar's white light, their beards dripping over his elbow. Inside, Riley's already hooked a tahr buck over the drain. The guests, disembarked, look on. The bird's still giving off a swell of fervid heat. Dino won't winch it the thirty feet into the hangar until season's end. He's clambering around inside it collecting firearms and ammunition, head-set collaring his neck.

"You should've seen the stag," says the man who paid. He takes a bottle off Loyola's tray.

"Twelve-pointer," says his brother. "Broadsided him on a cliff."

"Prehistoric," says the wife. Her face is lit and lined by the fluorescents. Upon arrival, she'd exclaimed devoutly through the tour of the main lodge, the cabins, the green rocky pool, every glance out over the valley bowl. Down the trail, she admired the old barn's rack and ruin. Now she stands on the hangar's stained cement with sweat on her lip and navy mascara freckling the top of her cheekbone. She flashes wide eyes at Loyola. "Just breathtaking," she says, "All those creatures out there."

"Took a shot, anyway," the man says. "Went down most of that bluff on his feet. Spent an hour tracking him."

"Who knows," says the brother.

"Bad luck," says Loyola.

"We couldn't get down to the bottom," says the wife. "The cliff."

"Couldn't see a fucking thing." The man's shrivelled smirk. That red stag's an easy twelve hundred pounds. Antlers thick as ankles. Loyola remembers him. She's not a small woman, but if she stood at his feet and embraced his neck she wouldn't reach his withers. Her fingertips spread wouldn't span the tines of his crown. No trophy for a shot like that, all the glory's in the fall.

Dino blinks all the bird's little lights off, and carries an armful of slick black branches to the cage at the back of the hangar. He doesn't look at her as he passes. He replaces each rifle into its cradle, slides drawers around, bolts the lock.

Riley's already got the tahr half-naked, hide draping his knees. The paying man wants to do the chamois, so Dino hands him a skinner. Forelegs snap wet like live wood at the ankle. The pelts peel bloodlessly. Fat greases their hands. Loyola twists her own bottle.

"Never seen deer so huge," says the wife. This wife, who spent four hours in a helicopter with three men and an arsenal. She's had twenty years of this. She married a man who took her to the shooting range on their first date. She likes the soft muzzles so much she wants them in her home: clear eyes overlooking dark wood and grey slate.

"Biggest in the world," Loyola agrees around her bottle's lip. Her teeth, set in the ridges of the glass. The tray, cocked against her right hip.

Out in the yard, the dogs writhe around each other at the lit periphery. They aren't begging. Dino instructs the tourists without instructing them. They're experienced. They know how to slice a body hung from the anklebones so the offal balloons from the incision like a fawn's head. The organs slide over themselves to the cement. The drain runs. Dino has the discreet authority of a butler, the woolly presence of an uncle, and the guests don't notice his corrections. Riley finds the stereo and smudges a button with a finger to clatter the steel walls with guitar noise.

The wife is watching close enough that when the men laugh she laughs. Loyola hovers back in the open air. She'll have to get more beer. A smoky breeze sneaks down through the scrub pines from the peaks. The girl's emerged from the lodge. She steps like she's passing through an herb garden in those battered boots Dino brought her home in. Her hair might be alive. When she got out of the jeep she was wrapped in a scabby fur. Dino said, "You don't want

215

this," and peeled it from her shoulders as she twisted away. She pauses out past the dogs and their switching shadows. The hooked game jerk and spin under the lights. The heads hacksawed, lined up on the tool gurney like they might want to watch. The girl cranes.

Loyola crosses the yard, tray dangling, and the girl lets her approach. Loyola does not touch the bare shoulders as she says, "Go to bed. Honestly."

"Don't you hunt elk?"

"Whatever the license is for."

"That's what they wanted, though, right?"

"Bad shot," says Loyola.

The room they installed her in last night is just a few knocks down from Loyola's own door. These are extra rooms, upstairs, barely used because the guests all prefer the privacy of the cabins. There's a black iron queen with a blue quilt and a slit-eyed bobcat treed over the mantel. Last night Loyola gave the girl a nightgown, a toothbrush, and pointed out the white towels in the en suite. This morning, when she found the girl in the kitchen before dawn, she handed over spare clothes.

The quilt is rumpled in circles as if one of the dogs had napped in the centre of the compass rose. The girl goes straight to the window. In the white light of the hangar's mouth, the men stand like fangs.

Dino drives the guests out the next morning, the jeep loaded with racks and meat. Loyola finds the wife's shampoo and conditioner in the first cabin's steam shower. They smell like flowers she doesn't recognize, invasive exotics, but they're not so expensive the woman will call and ask for them to be mailed. Loyola can take them back to her room. They're for redheads and she's redhaired, though not like the wife with her layers and shades.

She sprays every surface with disinfectant. They left condom wrappers on the bedside table, the wastebasket a foot away. The paying man was smiling as she refilled his coffee four times this morning, and as he thanked her for her hospitality in the drive. She drags the bed sheets off the mattress, has to crawl across the king's width to pluck the fitted corners up. His smell hides in the linen like a body in a blind. Chemical cedar. The wife's copper filaments wire the pillowcases like the remains of a gutted radio. Loyola does not seek out the spots where they soaked the sheets through, but still, she can smell what they left rising from the bale in her arms.

The only thing she finds in the brother's cabin is a tip in American singles. She pockets them. This far into the season they're still in the red, and the couple thousand from these three will splinter fast. In the lodge, she pushes the sheets into the laundry, pours bleach, and goes to the kitchen to stack half a dozen roast-beef sandwiches.

Now the sun's up, soaking the mountaintops and green-heating the trees. The helicopter gleams on its pat of asphalt. The paint scratches have been polished away. She finds Riley under the hooks in the hangar, sluicing the concrete. He's too lazy to scrub. The air in here is cool with silt, paint, old meat. He throttles the water before taking a sandwich. He eats it with unwashed hands, the creases in his knuckles dark.

"You seen Stein?" she asks.

"Barn, maybe."

The dogs follow the roast beef on her plate. Down the switchblade trail, dried hot with rusted juniper and pinesap, to the barn. Come upon it from above and it's a hag's house: steep-pitched, stitches of paint on the leeside. There's a paddock where she and Dino used to keep the horses when they ran the place by saddle. But it wasn't a barn originally. At some point, Dino's forebears lived inside. Dino's been saying they should buy a few auction-block nags. He says he misses the whickering at night. But Dino thinks money shows up as soon as you've spent it.

She ducks into the dust-pit paddock and as she nears the unlatched doors Stein slides out.

"Morning." He's a skinny kid, short, the tip of a tattoo starting under his left ear. He's not breathing right. She looks at his greasy lips and guesses where the girl is.

He takes two sandwiches, one in each hand.

She says, "Riley's got that west gate yet."

Stein nods as he works his snake throat. Nods and swallows. Keeps nodding, swallowing.

The doors creak and the girl joins them. Her eyes flick to the trees, the paddock corners, the sharp ears of the dogs, Loyola. She's wearing Loyola's dress: blue with white flowers, pearly-buttoned. Those boots, haydusted now, predictably.

"Morning," she smiles.

Stein closes his eyes against them both, chewing.

Loyola has never seen him embarrassed. She tips the last of the sandwiches towards the girl. "Roast beef."

The sandwich is opened like a book. The girl eats one slice of bread while looking down at the old dog, who supplicates forward on his elbows. The younger dog crouches likewise, at an hour-hand angle but just back. The girl tilts her hand, and the meat and cheese hit the ground, slick as livers in the pine needles. The girl eats the other slice of bread—margarine, lettuce. The dogs stare, arrested in half-launch. The old one's saliva jewels in the dust six inches from the meat.

Loyola scratches her forehead, sweeps crumbs from the plate. The dogs don't blink, watch the girl's eyes for release.

Stein swallows one last time, wipes his hands on his pockets. "That's cruel," he says. Then he crosses the paddock, hoofs the bluff's hairpins up to the hangar. The girl turns her face to track him. The old dog passes a twitch to the younger one.

"Blow away in a stiff wind," Loyola says.

"I like them like that."

Loyola snorts.

"All wrist and ankle." The girl rocks to her toes, swings her arms to stretch, and follows him.

At her first step, the dogs lunge. The old dog for the meat and the young dog for the old. The old dog twists to run and fight at once, drops the meat, pisses on the ground. He thrashes on his spine in the dirt with the younger on his throat. The younger is snarling and doesn't let go until Loyola boots him off. White fur pink, black fur oiled wet. The old dog spiders into the pines. The younger, wet-muzzled, snaps the meat and it's gone.

Dino comes back after three. He drove the tourists all the way to the airport instead of just to town, which is all they're supposed to get with the package. He almost always does that, unless he can't stand the people, and there aren't many people he can't stand.

He's brought back groceries and two tanks of fuel. They usually tip him in hundreds. Loyola shelves cans while he opens a beer and eats the sausage she's sliced for him.

"I was thinking she'd be good on the front desk. Answer the phone, greet them, get them settled."

"What desk," Loyola says from the pantry.

"You know what I'm saying."

"Sure," Loyola agrees, pulling her bag of salt forward on the shelf, tucking a new one behind it. "Pretty smile."

Dino is silent and Loyola takes the cans off the counter. She ferries two loads before Dino says, "You think she's got much else?"

Loyola lifts her eyebrows at the vinegar. He was supposed to be picking up the repaired sump pump the night he brought her home. No report on where he found her. Gas station, truck stop, diner, ditch. Barelegged, with blades for calves. Veins like spring rivulets down the backs of her brown hands. Right now, the girl's asleep in the sunlight by the pool, the younger dog in sprawl nearby. She's obviously healthy. Fast blood. Curved hamstrings like she was built for flight. She would've asked him for a light or a phone call. Dino would've had to offer more. He offered Loyola a meal, which she declined, and when his came she ate half of it with grimed fingers. She remembers onion rings, a screwdriver. He drove a rusted-out Ford back then.

He says, "She mention family to you?"

"Not to me."

"We could give her a hand," he says.

"Of course," she says.

He watches her for a while, swirling his bottle. She plucks four tomatoes from the basket. He turns on the radio. She halves, quarters them. Flicks a burner on. Why did she start cutting these? He looks out the side door to the hangar. He goes outside. Loyola twists the stove off again.

The girl picks herself up off the stone terrace when Loyola steps out into the sun. Red seams on the flats of her arms and thighs where the rough rock pressed her. The urns alongside the pool are just nameless grocery-store annuals, whatever was on sale. Up here the sun is so close it thins the air dry. The stalks give up their dead easily: Loyola plucks browned florets and tucks them to decompose in their own roots. She tips water into them.

The girl trails after her. Her hair is clean now. It's the colour of woods before foliage. She points her face at everything in turn. Loyola pulls a limp clump that leaves her fingers sticky and purpled. The girl snaps off something and rattles the roots doing it. She doesn't look at it, just drops the golden head on the stone. Loyola moves on to the next. The girl murders another.

"I brought you this," she says.

Loyola looks over her shoulder. The girl opens her palm. A twig. A rough-barked stick thick as a finger bone and grey with witch's beard.

"Magic powers," the girl promises. One eyebrow up, smirking.

Loyola takes it.

"You should use it," the girl advises. She pulls a plant whole from the soil, roots dripping mud.

"Thank you," says Loyola. She slides it into her breast pocket.

The girl follows her back to the faucet. The younger dog's sucked up some new scent trail and whips back and forth in the lodge's shadow, rushing their legs. His fur is wet.

"What did he do with my pelt?" says the girl.

"It's in the rifle locker at the back of the hangar."

The dog yelps once, thrilled. The girl's fingers shred the flower in her hands. She's standing very close. "What about yours?"

Loyola picks up her watering can. "He burnt mine," she lies.

The sound the girl makes isn't audible, it's too deep in the lungs. Her pink mouth. She reaches for Loyola's wrist, but Loyola's stepped away.

The next party is four men. They're staying the weekend; they've booked three flights in the bird. They're licensed for a small massacre. When they climb out of the jeep Dino names everyone, but Loyola lets the burning wind off the peaks take the sounds.

Dino introduces the girl alongside Loyola and Riley while Stein moves luggage into the cabins. Stein's been loitering after the girl. He and the old dog always at the edge of sight, ready to disappear. He doesn't come to sit at dinner, or around the hearth in the great room when the sun steps behind the mountains.

Through the plate glass, the valley is a thick fur of pines, piebald with broadleaves and slit by the river. Loyola serves beer, coffee, whisky. The sun appears again, then moves behind the next peak. Every poplar for miles is a steeple with leaves like lit windows.

The girl sits off in one of the solitary armchairs cornered beneath a herd of twelve-tined heads. Their expressions vary: some have artful, alert ears and lifted chins, but the elder faces are dull as barn mares. Their dusty eyeballs. The girl keeps her bottle full between her bare knees. She is silent. She may be listening. That's fine, the men don't want her to speak. They just like an audience sometimes, until they don't. At that point Loyola gets tired and stands. "Are you tired?" she asks the girl.

They climb the open stairs together. The men are watching. The girl murmurs, "What about the one with glasses?"

The men are talking about pilot licenses. One of them's an air-traffic controller. One is building a floatplane in his garage.

"It's his credit card on file," is the only thing Loyola knows about him.

"Which cabin?"

Loyola bites her smile.

"I bet he thinks I'm your daughter."

"Probably."

The men are laughing.

"He'll like that," the girl says.

The men are still laughing.

The girl jostles her shoulder against Loyola's. At the top of the stairs, the row of doors. Loyola in one, the girl in hers. At the end of the gallery is Dino's. Beneath them in his armchair Dino is telling about flying through last year's whiteout, two bears dead in the cage.

The girl says, "So it's elk tomorrow."

"Or something."

"Can I go with them?"

Loyola shrugs. She asked, once.

"I could walk," the girl says.

Loyola leans her shoulder against the frame. "There's a trailhead past the river. Up Sawback. We could drive part of it, walk the rest."

"You want to come?" says the girl.

"I want to see his body."

The girl blinks. If she were the least bit human her wet eyes would be full of pity.

When Dino comes upstairs it's late, black in the valley and in the house. Loyola's been sitting in the glow of her little lamp. She's fingered the bark off the twig the girl gave her. He isn't drunk enough to stumble. He's led the guests to their cabins. She cracks her door when he's close. Then she widens it.

She never sees his broad face anymore, she never touches his grey hair that's too long. He's always had gun-dog eyes and she puts her nose to the collar of his shirt so he can't look at her. He smells like he's always smelled. He never stopped smelling this way, but he stopped letting her get close enough to know it. It's painful, how familiar he is. Her memories are accurate, even if they're used ragged.

"What?" he says. She stays close under his chin, out of sight.

She kisses his throat. With his hands inside her shirt his mouth becomes less inhospitable. She is steady and silent. She used to voice eagerness. Then she learned to conceal herself in the underbrush, let him track her down. Lately, she's been waiting months, seasons; this dry summer at least.

The girl's little stick, lost on the bedspread, jabs her. She'd rescue it from snapping under them, but her hands are busy. She arranges them, moves on him. He grips to slow her down but she refuses. He comes loudly, even though next door the girl is or is not listening.

Loyola pulls away as he takes in air. She could lay herself down beside him like she used to and let all his circling mongrel thoughts thicken the air. Instead, she brushes away the snapped halves of the twig. In her bathroom she runs water like she's killing his scent, clearing the mess. But she doesn't step under the jet. She stands, lock-kneed on the tile, with him all over her.

Outside, there are bodies under the trees. Split hooves and missing skulls, bones jawed open by opportunists. She's found them deep in underbrush or at the foot of high places. She walks whole days. She finds a few every season. Never any antlers. She can't tell. She couldn't say for sure. Who else would come all this way but their guests, their dogs.

When she comes back he's gone, draped her pelt over the quilt, fur down, a skin waiting to wrap her. She's always been free to go.

At breakfast, the men are mouthy over coffee. The one in glasses is grinning his stupid secret away. The girl doused him with herself. He must think he split her open. Dino is all anecdotes and wisdom. He smiles at Loyola when she refills his mug. She walks back and forth, bringing hot things and removing what's finished.

In the kitchen she fills a cooler with sausages, cheese, hard-boiled eggs, bread. Dino comes in. He strokes her waist. He puts his nose to the back of her neck and breathes against her vertebrae. He kisses her skin.

She stays still until he goes. Then her knees sag. Her mouth opens. She folds against the cabinets, forehead to the wood, battered in the chop.

In his room, she does not touch anything or inhale. This room, the master, built when they first conceived of this life. Not horses but helicopters. Rifles and racks for tourists. They sold twelve strong mares too cheap at auction. They didn't need all the extra acres of conifers. Loyola slept in this wide bed. She crept from it every morning to percolate the coffee. He's left it immaculate.

The spare key for the gun locker is jumbled with some others—the generator shed, the jeep—in a drawer.

The girl comes with her to the locker, a chain-link partition at the back of the hangar. Loyola skims the black barrels. The girl goes straight for her pelt, stuffed into an empty shelf. It has no arms or buttons, no collar. It's short-haired, rough, built on summer. In this light it's the colour of dead leaves. Its underside is wet-white with grease, as if he peeled it off her an hour ago. The girl folds it to her chest, bends her face down to rub against it.

Stein and the dogs stare at them when they come out into the yard. The side door hangs open. The sun's been up for an hour, but the light's still choked pink, the valley hazy with forest fires. Later, in the worst of it, they'll all wake bleeding from the nose, desiccated, and Loyola will wash bloody sheets every morning.

Stein's mouth moves as he calls to them. The old dog wags low, once.

As Loyola turns the engine, the girl rolls her neck to look at the lodge, the cabins, the flowers lining the pool. She doesn't see Stein where he stands. "Slaughterhouse," she mutters, leaning back into her seat.

Down the valley, across the river to the trailhead. The path is dry, scraping along at the spine of the Sawback peaks, a root-bound stepladder climb between aspen stands. It's not quiet. There's a roar. The red stags don't bugle like birds, they make a meat-eater's sound of want.

One of them sounds, miles off.

Close, an answer from a larger set of lungs, a fuller-maned throat.

The girl's grin widens. Loyola keeps climbing. The girl bounds ahead, hair sweating to her skin.

Loyola keeps her eyes on the cliffs, and the bottoms of the cliffs, for his branched antlers. He'll be his own grave-marker. They found him where he grazed. And the shot, if it hit, hit the hollow behind his shoulder blade. He tipped starboard, overcorrected, then toppled. His land- slide body. His feet at gallop down the shale. She'll find his corpse at the bottom, splayed by petty birds. Or else he walked away.

When they reach a bluff, a scoop neck between peaks yawning east over the foothills, they stop. The girl picks at her buttons. The borrowed jeans come off, the wet shirt. She's stout, naked. Her sunburnt clavicle. She holds up her fur, and flaps it. In the smoke it's roan red, speckled down the haunches, paler in the belly. She turns into it, smiling as she shivers its fatty lining over her shoulders. The forelegs ribbon down between her breasts. Loyola reaches to pull the girl's hair out from under the pelt, and smoothes the lock down over one shoulder.

A stag roars eastward. Loyola jerks. That was his voice. The one who fell, or didn't. There he is.

Beside her, the yearling doe with her long neck and soft muzzle flicks her ears and stamps her four fresh legs. She's taller than a thoroughbred, black eyes already dis- tant with alien concerns. She steps into the trees, crackling dead sticks, branches brushing her flanks and waving in her wake. She moves slowly, but she's gone.

The road back to the lodge is rutted with smoke. The dirt widens into the drive before the rippled skin of the hangar. Loyola comes around and the young dog runs the older right under her wheels. His body is a jolt. She stops. Kills the engine. The younger wheels away, shouting.

The old dog is dying as she gets to him. His feet scrabble but it's just his broken back finishing off. She touches his swivelling ears, then carries him to the hangar. She has to check. She heaves him up to hang and slits him to drip. The younger is hiding. There are a hundred places. The woods, or under the veranda. She follows the smell of him down the trail into the old barn and finds him in the box stall, backed up under the feed trough, growling like a meat grinder. He is wet-mouthed and serrated. His throat tears rabid threats. He'll chase her bleeding through the woods. He'll find her by her screams. He'll pulp her soft face and pull open her throat. He'll drag her down and dye his muzzle in her rib-cage. Has he ever killed anything? It doesn't matter.

She puts the skinner into him under the edge of his skull and he shakes down to the hay, eyes straining at her. She carries him, soaking hot, back to the hangar to heave him up beside the other. Her mouth is dry. She is panting. She splits his belly, lets his lungs, bowel, stomach slop on the shop floor, cuts off his paws and peels his fur face. She flaps his bloody pelt off his body. His dog body. Nothing but dog.

Vazova on Love

i. *Zona*

I am not supposed to be here, but I'm afraid he'll die if I leave. Outside, the wind is snowless and histrionic over the hills, across the harbour. Time disgusts me. 49,993/50,000ths of sunlight could be darkness, but the idiot eye's too slow to see it. If I don't move from this spot, feet on tile, gut churning with espresso, time should stop. The gas stove clicks but doesn't light. No, it's the other way around, one moves faster to slow time. Even if we run, black blades across the northern shore of nightfall, we'd still be convicts. I linger here, and in the other room he coughs and I don't know what would be worse: if he was killed here now with me, or if I left and came back to find him killed. The latter, the latter is much worse. I require him, now, for my project. I am burning away the lead and iron. I will not go unless he comes with me. I don't remember wishing for him, but it's why one comes here. He will not lock the door. I require him. The clock changes its numbers every time I look back.

ii. *Murmansk*

He was the Russian desk, so when he retired, at thirty-two, to take the defense contractor's money, he was assigned to a concrete apartment block monitoring a camera for eight months of twelve-hour shifts. He watches what it watches. You imagine spies come here to kill people. There could be arsons, executions in the port, but the only things he verifies—the camera to report, the man to verify—are the names and numbers on the container ships that whale through the weakling harbour ice. A master's degree. Six years in the infantry. A dog left behind with a brother who's divorcing his own wife. The government pays the contractor to pay him a hundred twenty thousand a year. He reads a lot of Bulgakov, Gogol, and that paranoiac Krzhizhanovsky. Two missile boats lie half-submerged at the entrance to the harbour. False dawn doesn't plink the sky until noon.

iii. *Uncertainty v Certainty*

His door is never locked. I do not ask who came before me. I keep imagining summer here. The next woman could walk in at any moment, but for once there are no other women. I look down from the front window to see no queue formed in the slush-marsh street. Women in muskrats and heavy wool, thin women with dark hair and glassy eyes. By men, for men. Do not compare yourself to them, angels. I know we're all more familiar with angry women. Just because a woman's been sent doesn't mean she's been sent to kill. There is no comparison, not in this language. I'm here to verify. Summer here would breathe. Light all day. The doors propped open, following the sun in a circle around the apartment: front room, left room, back room. Leaves green and matted with a sudden, warm rain. Leaves. The sounds of him carry through the air, from front room to left room to back. In my sleep, he tells me, I yelped his name.

iv. *Crystallization*

At first I watched him at his desk, watching his screen. He hunched two floors above me in this concrete pile. My fish-eye lens angled up at him from within a scowling electrical outlet. He was so handsome, our twelve hours would pass too quickly. The lines of his kindness sloped from his eyes when he smiled. The only time he smiled was when he'd walk into the library, where I wore glasses. He touched my shoulder as he asked a low question in Norwegian. His ears looked roundly boxed. His ears have crystallized my notion of perfection in ears. At my desk in my apartment I ate salt fish on salt crackers. I can seem shy and kind. My shifts watching him stretched to sixteen, twenty hours. I knew when he was shitting and when he was sleeping. I imagine the container ships are full of beach sand, hardcovers, national flags shrink-wrapped in plastic. Heroin. More angry women. That's a joke. I'd tie back my hair, smooth my collar, put on my glasses, and smile at him from behind the library desk. The library: dirty white linoleum; chairs with sharp, metal feet. He disdained Tolstoy. He chose to speak Norwegian so he'd sound like the usual kind of foreigner. I couldn't speak English to him for obvious reasons.

I read that both his Serbian and French are flawless, yet here he is. He watches what his camera watches. When he masturbates, so do I. The boats don't drift. I imagine he's imagining me behind my desk or under it or bent over it. By men, for men. Anger is insanity when a woman performs it. His body is taut. He winks at me when I see him in the salt-mine stairwell of our apartment block. He runs up and down the flights for an hour after every twelve-hour shift. Every few days I allow myself to encounter him there: soaked, dripping hatred. Yet he winks at me; we collude. Our hatreds are our own. At minus fifty, the harbour is a salt flat with a war-cloud of snow flying across its plain, but the ice is never as real as it looks.

v. *Nighthawk*

I requisitioned an explosive-gas and carbon-monoxide detector and planted it behind his couch. But how will he know what the alarm means when it sounds? Don't die in your sleep when I'm speaking to you. Don't die in a hellfire. Instead of watching him watch what his camera watches through my camera now I just watch him. When I am finished with this project, will I see a vision of God's face, or a beatified border guard's? I've entered here with a bottle of champagne, with a brick of coffee, with three pairs of fake passports, with three beers, with a bottle of vodka, with two pastries, with a bag of gummies, with a box of gingerbread cookies, with four bananas, with my favourite two hundred pages of *Anna Karenina*, with a hundred thousand paper rubles. He purchased a larger coffee press. If we do this right we'll live forever in each other. He leaves a key in my coat pocket. I take this to mean I should go and lock the door on my way out, and then return when he is not present, but I have ceased to enter, and also the door is never locked. When he looks at me my neon blood pistons up and down my arms and legs. At night his eyes glint while we stare across the dark to each other. The key is useless to me. What if he dies?

vi. *Happy New Year*

He says in Russian, quietly, and his accent is fine so I don't know why he's spent all these weeks pretending to be Norwegian, "Would you have a drink with me?" I have to go shopping. I wait in my apartment, wash my holes. I watch him change from shirt to shirt and lock his own door, then I lock away my equipment. I put it behind the garbage can and cleaning supplies under the kitchen sink. I imagine leaving it out so he'd know immediately without my lying. Lipstick. We share a bottle in my living room, which belonged to an old woman with a black mouth before I took it. The chairs are wooden, the blankets pink. I bring him salt fish, and caviar. I can seem attentive and loving. The women up here have a reputation for shrieking when they wake up, gutted. It makes sense. We've all poured ourselves empty into someone. Which wish was granted? He kisses me beside the sink, where I'm pouring more liquor. I'm drunk. I'm not drunk. In that moment I stopped being angry and never started again. Pain ceased.

vii. *Autobiography*

Doubt is dead, yet evil is bearded and growing fat with paranoia. If I went out I'd catch it bedevilling the bars of this country. I slept beside it for all those years, woke and made the sweat-wet bed each morning. My project is atonement. Come inside me while I bleed and let our humours runnel my legs and let that be like raising a daughter together. I anoint myself twice a day. You angels, please beg for me in your hall. The fires of purification melt iron that beads from my pores. I have lied to every one of you, in small ways and large. I have used every detail for my own purposes. Yes, I have walked into unlocked rooms and executed the men who waited for me there. I have soothed evil in its night terrors. I abase myself. I beg you. Lead pours from my mouth. My project is reconciliation.

viii. *Ships Sink*

"You're not from here."

"Is anyone?"

"Yes," I say. "Not me though. Either."

"You've come for work?" we ask, simultaneously.

"Shipping," we both say, simultaneously.

"I volunteer at the library, otherwise I'd die of loneliness," I add, remembering.

"That pig barn should get a book," he says.

Our lies clunk together like skulls. He hasn't been a good liar in years, I bet. I've always been, but I don't have the heart for this.

"Would you rather speak English?" I say, in English.

His lungs stop lifting. I raise my head from his chest to look at him. My glasses are on the floor beside the mattress. The mattress has its starched floral sheet and its wool blanket. Both reek with all the soap I used washing them. Now the sheet's creased, wet. I've been meaning to buy a second sheet to slide between the blanket and the skin. For once I am warm enough to lie uncovered. Six years in the infantry. Since I've uncovered him, should he murder me? Perhaps that's why there's no line of women. Perhaps the container ships are full of their corpses. Again, a joke. No one kills a woman for the same reason we'd kill a man.

"Is my accent that bad?" he says.

"It's excellent," I say.

"So is yours," he says.

"Thank you."

No, he's here to make sure the camera's red light glows. The rotten ice in the harbour disintegrates invisibly. He checks the time. Our shinbones grate as he takes himself away. He goes back to his apartment. This is the first and only time I'll allow that. I pull my equipment from under the sink and reactivate my view of him. He picks up the phone. My phone rings.

"Come up for dinner," he says. This is when I requisition the bottle of champagne.

My phone rings again, "All good?" says my line agent.

"Yes," I say. I'm not even sure what the question that needs answering is. If I hadn't acquired this apartment myself, direct from that black-mouthed old Tatiana, I would wonder if they'd wired it. What's in the shipping containers? All the world's questions in a seething oort cloud, purely theoretical planetesimals, grumbling intestinally, waiting to be asked. It occurs to me they don't need a physical wire just to listen to my phone. Then it occurs to me he could just die. At any time, he could die.

ix. *Ex Zona*

In the night I am dead asleep but I dig a talon into his

navel. He wakes and pushes me away. I don't remember what I wanted. Would I pour in the molten black of myself? Would I crawl into his cavity and make a shrine of us? I see there is no end. I see where I ripped a piece of his shirt, or him, and didn't comment or apologize. I lost the Krzhizhanovsky he gave me before I learned why the eye is so stupid 49,993/50,000ths of the time. I'm hungry. I cannot work on my project and write this, simultaneously. It results in reversals. I see the cracks flicker. The sun's beams are stretched so taut they snap. Angels, what you saw as sunlight was just suffering. What did you come here to wish for? If anyone were to execute him it's likeliest to be me. Two floors down my phone is ringing. We'll blind and kill these cameras. We'll leave now. No one needs to come for us. Everyone knows what the end looks like until the end never comes.

Acknowledgements

Thank you to the many good souls who read many versions of these stories at many glorious assemblages: the Alpha Stones, the Night Ladies, and Puny Times Gallery's Own Friday Night Fiction Club, most especially Kristyn Dunnion, Jani Krulc, Sarah Burgoyne, Madeleine Maillet, Hilary Bergen, Yann Geoffroy, William Vallieres, Jessi MacEachern, Alonso Gamarra, Kasia Juno, Jeff Noh, Jon Shanahan, Susan Sanford Blades, and Kira Procter. Lauren Turner wrote across the table. Dave Guimond wrote in the other room. Frances Key Phillips talked me through everything then edited the shit out of all of it.

Thank you to the editors and magazine staff who first published these stories: Gerard Beirne and Mark Jarman at *The Fiddlehead*, Vicki Lawrence and Jonathan Freedman at *Michigan Quarterly Review*, Adrienne Perry at *Gulf Coast*, Madeleine Maillet at *Cosmonauts Avenue*, Robin Richardson at *Minola Review*, Mark Laliberté at *CAROUSEL*, Emily Donaldson at *Canadian Notes &*

Queries, Pamela Mulloy at *The New Quarterly*, and G.C. Waldrep at *West Branch*.

Thank you to the peerless John Metcalf for being the wizard of my life. Emily Donaldson's dazzling razorblade excised all my inanity. Casey Plett is my idol and Jonny Flieger is my soul twin. Meghan Desjardins, Dan Wells, Chris Andrechek, and everyone at Biblioasis have done endless work on this book for little reward besides my inappropriate and poorly timed expressions of love.

Thank you to the Conseil des arts et des lettres du Québec and the Canada Council for the Arts for providing the financial support late capitalism never will. Thank you to the Banff Centre for both the artist and the staff cards. Thank you to Sarah Selecky. Thank you to Mathieu Drouin and the Crystal Mathletes for giving me a home. Thank you to Genghis and Montreal Improv for fixing my personality. Thank you to NOASS Arts + Culture Project in Riga, Latvia, for the eyrie and the pigeon corpse and for my dearest Kate Zilgalve, who gave this book its name.

Thanks to Alison Carpenter for the shelter. Thanks to Anna Harland for sending me on my way. Thanks to Brooke Bentham for believing in me. Thanks to Sasha Frere-Jones for recording over the bad tapes. Thanks to Owen, Helen, and Olive for holding the fort. Thank you, Stu & Ingy. Thank you, Allie. Thank you Cathy Sullivan, and all the other librarians of my life.

About the Author

PHOTO: ADAM MICHIELS, 2016

Paige Cooper was born and raised in the Rocky Mountains. Her stories have appeared in *The Fiddlehead*, *West Branch*, *Michigan Quarterly Review*, *Gulf Coast Online*, *Canadian Notes & Queries*, *The New Quarterly*, *Minola Review*, *Cosmonauts Avenue*, and have been anthologized in *The Journey Prize Stories* and *Best Canadian Stories*. She lives in Montreal.